Suddenly Mine

ALSO BY KATIE EVERGREEN

APEX BILLIONAIRES' CLUB
Book 1: Suddenly Tempted
Book 2: Suddenly Desired
Book 3: Suddenly Mine

SUDDENLY
Mine

KATIE
EVERGREEN

Choc Lit
A JOFFE BOOKS COMPANY

Revised edition 2025
Choc Lit, London
A Joffe Books company
www.choc-lit.com

First published as *My Christmas Billionaire* in 2018

This paperback edition was first published
in Great Britain in 2025

Cover art by Alexandra Allden

ISBN: 978-1781899137

To the daydreamers and the hopeless romantics — thank you for believing in love stories, never stop rooting for a happy ending.

CHAPTER 1

MERRY

Merry Sinclair's backside had frozen to the window as she slept. Again. Not her skin, thankfully — nobody needed frost burn on their delicate bits — but the brushed cotton pyjamas that had failed to keep her warm while she slept. She wriggled enough to unstick them and tried not to wince at the dampness as they sprang back on her butt.

Her room was so small she had no choice but to push her bed against the glass or the door would get wedged on its way open. But every winter was the same and their landlord had refused to do anything about it because, quote, "your apartment is rent-controlled and I'm practically paying you to live there."

She tried to summon the will to reach for her phone. Not because she was eager to face the day, but because there was a very real chance she'd slept through her alarm. When she finally peeled her arm from the duvet and found her phone face down and dead, it confirmed her suspicions. Her breath misted visibly as she sat up, and she muttered a short, heartfelt curse into the biting air.

1

The worst part wasn't even the cold or the lack of sleep. It was that she was about to be late to a job she didn't even want, for a shift she hadn't exactly agreed to. December hours at Carroll's Department Store were like being drafted into Christmas bootcamp — nobody asked if you were available, they just slapped your name on the rota in red pen and dared you to complain. Merry couldn't afford to complain.

She scrambled out of bed, bare feet hitting the ice-cold floor. Her slippers had vanished, probably into her roommate's room along with half of her wardrobe. Showering at supersonic speed, she pulled on jeans and a jumper and stomped across the freezing apartment, each breath a visible puff. A lesser woman might have cried. Merry just muttered an impressive string of expletives under her breath as she made for the kitchen. Coffee would save her.

She flicked on the ancient kettle — her coffee machine had broken a few weeks back — and grabbed her favourite chipped mug from the shelf. It was the one with the faded *I heart NY* printed on it, the only souvenir she'd ever allowed herself when she first moved to the city, when she was still naive enough to believe in new beginnings and happy-ever-afters. She opened the fridge door and stopped. It was bare. No milk, no orange juice, no butter. Just a half-empty jar of pickle relish and what looked suspiciously like a middle school science experiment growing on the cheese.

Merry closed her eyes, breathed and reached into the bread bin instead. She'd stashed an emergency two-pack of almond croissants in there yesterday, a little payday treat to make the mornings marginally less bleak. But that, too, was empty. Just a crumpled brown paper bag dusted with almond flakes was left squashed in the corner.

She was still staring at it in silent devastation when her roommate, Clare, called out from down the narrow hall.

"Morning, Mer. Hey, could you grab some groceries on your way home? I'm slammed with work today. Absolute nightmare."

Merry turned slowly, the rage starting as a gentle simmer somewhere behind her eyes. Groceries, right, because obviously she had all the time, money, and willpower in the world to navigate the bodega at 7 p.m., mid-December, after a long day on her feet. Before she could answer with a resounding no, Clare's bedroom door cracked open a few inches. A halo of soft golden fairy lights framed her perfectly tousled blonde hair and impossibly perky face.

"I'm out of oat milk," Clare added. "And, like, actual food. Love you."

She blew Merry a kiss and disappeared back inside, the door clicking shut. And it wasn't long before what could only be described as enthusiastic, definitely non-PG moaning emanated from her room. Merry stood frozen in the kitchen, mug dangling limply from her fingers. She stared at the empty fridge and the brown paper croissant bag, then, placing the mug down very gently on the counter, she turned on her heel and stomped towards the door, pulling her pom-pom beanie low over her face. If she didn't leave right now, there was a very real chance she'd be arrested for throwing a pickle jar at Clare's head.

By the time Merry made it outside, her hair had frozen slightly at the ends where she hadn't dried it. The wind slapped her cheeks and pinched her nose and the constant drizzle wormed its way through her duffle coat. The subway was delayed, and when it finally arrived it was packed tighter than a Christmas turkey in foil. She squeezed herself in beside a man with three shopping bags and mouth-breathed the whole way there because the journey smelled like feet. Every jolt of the train pressed her closer to the window until she emerged on to Fifth Avenue with a crick in her neck.

The avenue was a riot of lights, the city dressed to the nines for Christmas. Shop windows exploded with colour and glamour. Merry breathed out a long cloud of steam and felt her shoulders hitch. God, she hated Christmas.

She tilted her face up into the sleet, her cheeks prickling from the cold and her nose already numb. Somewhere across the street, a department store window burst into life, a giant mechanical Santa ho-ho-hoing and waving his mittened hands. On cue, Bing Crosby floated out from hidden speakers, crooning about white Christmases and mistletoe.

Merry sighed, stuffed her gloveless hands deeper into her pockets and trudged on towards Carroll's, which stood across the street like a glittering monolith to Christmas cheer. Carroll's was one of the most famous department stores in the world. And it was most famous for being *the* place to shop during the holidays. People streamed in from Fifth Avenue from morning until night, from Halloween to New Year's, marvelling at the giant Douglas fir that stood in the wide atrium, decked with over ten thousand fairy lights and a bedazzling golden star. It really was a sight to behold.

Now, though, the sight of it was almost enough to bring her to tears.

Her boots skidded slightly on the wet pavement as she pushed through Carroll's grand revolving doors and into the blast of warm, cinnamon-scented air. Instantly, Merry felt her bones start to thaw and her hair begin to frizz in the heat. She shook herself like a dog, straightened her coat and glanced around furtively. If she could just sneak to the staff elevators without being spotted, maybe she could clock in without adding another black mark to her already dismal record.

She edged her way along the marble-tiled floor, sticking close to the towering nutcracker soldiers and animatronic polar bears that guarded the atrium's tree. She was almost there when a voice cracked across the shop like a whip.

"Merry Sinclair."

Merry flinched and turned slowly to see Mrs Cradley standing there, clipboard clutched in her skeletal hands, eyes narrowed behind her gold-rimmed glasses. Merry mustered a smile, the kind she used when dealing with difficult customers or bad dates.

"Good morning, Mrs Cradley. Isn't it a lovely—?"

Mrs Cradley cut her off with a look sharp enough to etch glass. She stalked forward, her heels tapping furiously against the marble, and gave Merry a long, slow once-over that made her feel about three inches tall.

She could feel her bedraggled hair and damp duffle coat and drooping pom-pom hat. It wasn't a great look, even by Merry's modest standards.

At last, Mrs Cradley sniffed and tilted her chin up, as if the very sight of Merry offended her delicate sensibilities. "Carroll's," she said, her voice dripping with disdain, "expects more."

"Sorry," Merry muttered, shuffling to the elevators, but Mrs Cradley was already sweeping past her, barking orders at a nearby staff member about fingerprints on the display cases.

Inside the staff room Merry peeled off her sodden coat, opened her locker and pulled out her uniform — the mandatory Carroll's Christmas dress.

It was *technically* a dress, but felt more like a theatrical costume. The rich, velvet-red skater dress had a soft white faux-fur trim around the cuffs and hem, and was paired with thick green tights and a pair of polished black Mary-Jane heels that clicked when she walked, no matter how much she tried to sneak.

Grabbing the day's rota from the pinboard, she scanned it quickly, already bracing herself for bad news. Door duty. All day. She stuffed the paper back on to the board a little heavy-handedly. Door duty meant standing in the cold draft, welcoming shoppers into the building, handing out leaflets, smiling until her cheeks ached, and desperately hoping that the blast of warm air from the overhead heater would reach her before she turned into an icicle. It was possibly the worst job at Carroll's in December, but at least it came with the small blessing of not having to deal with angry customers or spilled lattes or, God forbid, Mrs Cradley herself.

Carroll's was already packed by the time she squeezed herself into position near the front doors, the atrium sparkling with fairy lights and ringing with the sound of Bing Crosby. She settled herself directly under the door heater, claiming the tiny sliver of warmth like a territorial cat, and plastered on the brightest smile she could manage.

And, against all odds, once she got into the rhythm of it, the day didn't seem quite so bad. She found herself lulled into a strange kind of hypnotic routine, handing out leaflets, dodging stampeding children, nodding politely at harassed parents and selfie-stick-wielding tourists. The hours slipped past faster than she would have believed after the catastrophic start to her morning.

"Welcome to Christmas at Carroll's! It's the happiest time of year!"

Merry Sinclair charged up her warmest smile, offering it to the young couple who had just walked through the door. She could see their relief as they caught the blast of hot air that blew down from the vent above, their cheeks glowing beneath their matching red pom-pommed reindeer hats.

She realised the young couple were standing there waiting for her to say something else, and she tried to make her smile even wider. It must have been too wide, though, because they started to edge away. Merry thrust a leaflet at them with one hand, using the other to nudge the itchy, oversized Christmas hat away from her eyes.

"Don't forget, if you spend over ten dollars you can get a free gingerbread cookie and hot drink in the restaurant," she said. "And enter the charity raffle for your chance to come to the legendary Carroll's Christmas Ball! Only four days left to go."

"Um . . . thanks," said the young woman, taking the leaflet between her thumb and forefinger like she'd been offered a mouldy banana. They hurried away, and Merry sighed.

It didn't matter how many lights they strung up, how many carols they blasted through the speakers, how many charity raffles and free cookies they handed out, Christmas to Merry still meant waiting for something that wasn't coming.

Three years ago, she'd believed Adrian, her ex, when he'd left for his new job on the West Coast, swearing he'd be back for Christmas. She'd roasted a turkey, decorated the apartment, even bought mistletoe like an absolute idiot. And she'd waited. And waited. And he never came.

6

The turkey burned because she was too distracted, then she couldn't bring herself to eat it alone. She'd sat at the wobbly kitchen table in her stupid sparkly dress, staring at the silent phone, while her roommate had loud, enthusiastic sex just one wall away. And somewhere across the country, Adrian had already moved on with someone new and better and had simply forgotten to tell Merry about it.

Since then, Merry had learned her lesson. Christmas magic was for other people or children or couples who had a future and absolutely not for people like her.

"Absolute knob!" she muttered under her breath. "I hate you."

"Whoa," said a voice from her side. "I'm sorry, I'll ask somebody else."

Merry swung around, her mouth open to apologise. The words didn't make it up her throat, though, because the man who was standing there literally took her breath away. He looked a little older than her, but there was a playful shine to his features that made him look younger. His eyes were the colour of chestnuts roasting on an open fire, and just looking at them made her feel like she was melting. The sharp angles of his jaw were covered in dark stubble, and his brown hair was still perfectly styled despite the fact he'd just walked in from the wind and the sleet. He smiled at her politely and started to walk away.

"Wait!" she blurted out. "I'm sorry!"

He turned back, and she wasn't sure if he smiled again or not because her hat slipped down over her eyes. She pushed it back up, managing to lose her grip on the leaflets she was holding. They fluttered down to the floor like snowflakes.

"Shit," she said. "Hang on."

She crouched down to retrieve the leaflets, noticing too late that the man was doing exactly the same thing. There was an audible *crack* as their foreheads knocked together.

"Ow!" she said, her hat slipping over her eyes again. This time she pulled it off, her copper-coloured hair delighted to be free and flying everywhere. "I'm really sorry," she said, blinking the tears from her eyes as she massaged her forehead.

The man was standing up again too, rubbing a red patch between his eyes.

"Are you okay?" she asked him.

Fortunately, he smiled, wincing a little. "Christmas shopping is a lot more dangerous than I remember it being," he said, his voice as rich and melodious as a Christmas crooner. "I'm sure this place used to be friendlier. First you say you hate me, then you try to knock me out!"

"I'm so sorry," she said. "I wasn't talking to you. I was thinking about . . . It doesn't matter. Somebody else. I really didn't mean to hurt you."

"That's some headbutt you have there," he said. "They should have you working security."

She laughed, grateful that the man was being so kind. She was on thin ice in the store as it was, and knocking a customer unconscious wouldn't exactly help her case with the management.

"I'm going in again," the man said, holding his hands up in warning. "I'm giving you plenty of notice this time."

He crouched down and scooped up the leaflets, handing them back to her.

"Thank you," she said. "I really appreciate it. Can I start over?"

She peeled a leaflet loose and handed it back to him.

"Free gingerbread cookie if you spend over ten bucks. A hot drink too. And if you buy a charity ticket you might even win the chance to come to the famous Carroll's Christmas Ball."

"They're still doing that?" he asked, glancing at the leaflet.

"Every year," she said. "This will be my first, but I hear they're amazing. One of the best parties in the city. It's in four days, so you'd better hurry!"

The man laughed, tucking the leaflet into the inside pocket of his faded lumberjack jacket, the soft flannel looking like it had seen better days. A woolly scarf, a little frayed at the ends, was looped loosely around his neck, and his dark jeans were well-worn, the kind that had moulded perfectly to his long, muscular legs.

Not exactly the image Carroll's usually catered to, he looked like he should be chopping wood on a Christmas card, not browsing the luxury counters of Fifth Avenue. Still, there was something about him — an easy confidence, a kind of rugged warmth — that made Merry's cheeks heat up all over again.

She looked up at his face to find that he was already watching her, his brown eyes crinkling with amusement and, unless she was imagining it, the faintest hint of a blush creeping into his cheeks too.

"Oh, um, sorry," she said. This was by far the most awkward encounter she'd ever had at work, and part of her wished the man would walk away so that she could stop making a fool of herself. But part of her didn't want him to leave because she was enjoying his company. "Are you looking for anything in particular?" she asked, just to keep him talking.

"No," he said. "Not as such. This isn't really a shopping trip."

"Oh." She looked over her shoulder to the enormous tree that glittered in the middle of the atrium. "Just sightseeing? It's well worth the trip. If you visit the restaurant on the eighth floor you can see all the Christmas lights of Fifth Avenue too."

He nodded and his smile wavered, as if there was something heavy weighing on his mind, and he looked a little lost. She reached out automatically to touch his arm, but pulled back at the last second. Management frowned on any kind of contact between staff and customers. There was a sudden flurry of cold air and noise as the doors opened, and a family walked in from outside. Three kids charged into the store, screaming, and Merry leaned past the man to hand a leaflet to their exasperated mother.

"Free gingerbread cookies," she said. "And Santa's grotto is on the tenth floor."

The woman thanked her and ran off after her kids. When Merry turned her attention back to the man he seemed to have recovered.

"I'm sorry," he said. "It's not you. It's just all this."

"Yeah, it's a little much, right?" she replied. "It's been like this since the day after Halloween."

"Seriously?" he said. "It gets earlier every year."

"I know!" said Merry. "Soon it's going to be Christmas all year round. Christmas Valentine's, Christmas Easter eggs, Christmas Independence Day. There will be no escape!"

He laughed, and it was such a warm, genuine sound that she laughed too. He nodded at her name tag, and she felt a sudden rush of embarrassment.

"I thought you'd be a fan of Christmas," he said. "Is your name really Merry?"

"Yes," she said.

"Short for Meredith?" he asked, and she shook her head.

"Nope, it's just Merry. Blame my parents, they called me that because they said I made them feel like every day was Christmas. You wouldn't believe the stick I got for it at school."

"I can guess," he said. "Believe it or not I had the same problem."

Before she could ask why, another large group of people walked through the door, forcing the man to take a step closer to her. He was tall, over six foot, and there was the most incredible scent drifting from him — part nutmeg, park citrus. Her body reacted before her brain did, with a stupid, instinctive flicker of heat that ran low and slow through her stomach.

She had to take a deliberate step back, pretending to adjust the stack of leaflets in her hands, because standing that close to him was starting to mess with her ability to form basic sentences.

"Don't get me wrong," she said. "I used to love Christmas. There's just something about this time of year that's so special, so much fun. But, you know, when you're all on your own like I am, it's . . ."

She put a hand to her mouth. Why did she always do this? No wonder men tended to give her a wide berth — she had a habit of throwing every little detail of her life at them within minutes of meeting.

"Sorry, way too much information."

"It's okay," the man said. "I totally understand. If you've got family around you, it's the happiest time of the year. But if you're on your own, it can be the loneliest."

"That's it," she said. "Exactly."

The song overhead changed to 'The Little Drummer Boy', and Merry shivered as another blast of cold air blew in from outside. The man didn't move. He was still standing there like he had all the time in the world, his hands tucked casually into the pockets of his worn jacket.

Merry swallowed. Maybe he was just being polite or waiting for someone. Or maybe he was just enjoying talking to her, and somehow that thought was even more terrifying. Because the longer she spoke, the more likely she was to say something so cringeworthy she'd spend the next six months reliving it at 3 a.m.

"So, what about you?" she asked. "Have you got family here in the city?"

"Yeah," he said, nodding. He looked like he was about to say more when somebody cleared their throat behind him. Merry's heart sank as Mrs Cradley stepped into view.

"Miss Sinclair, may I have a word?"

"I'm sorry, Mrs Cradley," Merry said, flapping a leaflet in the handsome man's face, even though he already had one. "I'm handing them out the best I can."

"This is neither the place nor the time for small talk," Mrs Cradley said, offering the man a dismissive smile that was almost rude. "I've been watching you for some time now. How many times do I have to tell you that we do not pay you to chat?"

"I was just . . ." Merry started, but she didn't have anything to add. She *was* just chatting. "I won't do it again."

"Excuse me," the man said, looking Mrs Cradley in the eye. He seemed to have straightened up, because he was even taller now than he had been moments ago. The force of his words made Mrs Cradley lean back, holding her clipboard up protectively. "This young woman was just helping me decide on what to buy my fiancée."

That hadn't been what they were talking about at all, and even though she was grateful to him for defending her, Merry's stomach turned unpleasantly when she heard that he was engaged.

"She was being extremely helpful, and I don't think she deserves to be treated like this. She's a credit to your store."

Mrs Cradley's eyes almost popped out of their sockets. She opened her mouth, then paused. She looked at the man, a strange expression on her bird-like face. Then she muttered something and hurried off into the perfume hall, using her clipboard to flap people out of the way.

"Wow," said Merry. "I'm so sorry that happened."

"You really don't have anything to be sorry about," the man replied. "She was completely out of order."

"Maybe." Merry gave a leaflet to another customer. Her hand was shaking, and she hoped that nobody would notice. She hated confrontation so much. All she wanted to do was curl up into a ball beneath the half-price saucepan sets across the aisle and hide there for the rest of her shift. "Maybe not. I do talk too much. I just forget myself sometimes."

"I like to talk," he said, and she smiled gratefully.

"So, do you want some advice on what to buy your fiancée?" she asked, trying to hide the disappointment in her voice. "There are some amazing pieces of jewellery on three, and we've got a new art department. If you like, I can show you around?"

"No, thank you." He opened his mouth as if to say something else, then glanced at his watch instead. "I'd better get on, my dad's expecting me."

"So you do have family," she said, smiling. "That's nice."

"Yes to family," he replied, looking like he wanted to add something more, but he stopped himself and Merry noticed a flash of sadness in his eyes.

"It was nice to meet you, Merry." He offered her his hand and she shook it eagerly.

"It was nice to meet you too—" She tilted her head expectantly.

"Christian," he said, taking the hint. "Have a very merry Christmas, Merry."

"You too," she replied, but as she watched him walk away — the way all men seemed to — she couldn't help but think that her own words of comfort were far from correct.

This holiday was going to be no better than the last.

CHAPTER 2

CHRISTIAN

Don't look back, Christian told himself. *Just don't look—*

He looked back, seeing the young woman who had greeted him. She was watching him go, and when he caught her eye she beamed another beautiful smile his way. Merry was an unusual name, but it fit her perfectly. She had to be in her early twenties, and everything about her seemed to suggest that she was merry and bright, just like the Bing Crosby song that had been playing a moment ago. She was dressed in the traditional Carroll's red dress, with green tights and shiny black heels that made her legs go on for miles. Her hair was a tumble of red curls that framed her face in a way that made it hard not to stare And her eyes, so bright green they were almost unreal, stood out even from across the lobby.

He waved at her, and she waved back, the little collection of leaflets exploding from her hand again. Even from here he heard her groan, and she almost took out another customer on the way down to collect them. He laughed gently, wondering if he should go back to help her. But he stopped himself. He wasn't here to speak to the greeters, no matter how pretty they were or how much he wanted an excuse to hang around.

14

The reason he was walking through the doors of Carroll's Department Store for the first time in five years was far more serious.

Christian sighed, looking around to get his bearings. The giant tree towered above him, reaching the balconies of the fourth floor and pouring out so much light that it almost hurt to look at it. There were hundreds of presents at its base, but Christian knew that all those perfectly wrapped boxes were empty and just for show. Kind of like how he felt now, standing here, showing up, but feeling hollowed out inside.

Taking a deep breath, he set off around the tree. The store was bursting full of people, young couples in matching Christmas jumpers and delighted children running rings around their parents, all of them laughing and smiling and shouting with excitement. How many times had he run screaming around this shop when he was a boy? He wished he could be as happy as they were, but it was a long time since he'd been able to enjoy the festive season. And now that he was back here, the chances of him enjoying this year's festivities were even slimmer. What he'd told Merry was true. Christmas was about family, and his family — the one person left in it, anyway — never made him feel very welcome.

He reached the elevator and rode it up with a group of high school kids who were hyped up on hot chocolate and marshmallows. They got off on the third floor, leaving him to ride to the top of the building alone as 'O Come All Ye Faithful' drifted from the speakers. He stepped off into the children's department on floor ten, making his way through the crowds gathered around Santa's grotto to the staff door right at the back of the building. There was a keypad there, and he typed in the number to open it — his date of birth. To his surprise, the light blinked red and the keypad bleeped angrily. He tried again, and as he was going for a third attempt the door swung open and Christian found himself face to face with somebody he hadn't seen in years.

"Christian Carroll," said Margot Miller, looking him up and down as if he was a rat that had scurried in from the street.

"I'd like to say it's good to see you, but we'd both know that would be a lie."

She was older now, but she looked almost exactly as he remembered her. Sharp navy suit, silver hair pulled into a tight twist and a gaze that could cut through steel.

"Margot." Christian nodded curtly. "The code has changed."

"A lot has changed," she shot back. "You'd know that if you hadn't abandoned ship."

Christian did his best to push the anger down into his stomach. He had known there was a chance Margot would still be working in the store, but he'd hoped he could get through today without seeing her.

"Is Dad here?" he asked. "He wanted to see me. He said it was urgent."

He'd received the message two days ago, at his base in the Philippine island of Rapu-Rapu. It had been the first contact from his dad in years, and something about the way it had been worded made it clear how serious it was. He'd packed up and flown home that night, and the thirty-six hours of travel were starting to take their toll. He rubbed his eyes, feeling like he could lie down right there and sleep for a week.

"He's here," said Margot. "I told him it was a bad idea to invite you, but you know how he is. There's no saying no to that man."

"Are you going to let me in, then?" Christian asked.

Margot smiled unkindly and didn't move, blocking him like a doorman.

"I warned your dad about bringing you back, but he insisted," she said, leaning close to deliver the ice-cold words directly into his ear. "Do not mess it up. Am I clear?"

"Crystal," Christian replied. "Believe me, I want to be here about as much as you want me to be. Just let me through."

Margot stood there for a moment more, then moved to the side.

"He's in the office," she said as he walked past. "And he's pretty angry."

That was nothing new. Lewis Carroll was as famous as his literary namesake, and as far as the world knew, he was the same gentle giant that appeared on the TV adverts every year dressed as Santa and ho-ho-hoing next to his giant Christmas tree. Only a few people had actually met the short-tempered, ruthless man behind the myth, and Christian knew the truth better than anybody. There was a good reason that his father was a billionaire, and it wasn't because he was as generous as Santa Claus. If anything, he was more like Ebenezer Scrooge — before the ghosts.

Christian walked past the staff locker room, reaching the office door. He paused, composing himself. Then he knocked.

"Who is it?" growled a familiar voice from inside.

Christian felt a rush of anxiety at the thought of seeing his dad again after so long. "It's me," he said, turning the handle and opening the door. "It's . . ."

He froze, thinking for a moment that he'd made a mistake. There was only one man in the bookshelf-lined room, sitting behind the same antique desk that had always been there, and framed by the huge window that looked out over the city. But it couldn't be his father. For one, he looked about half the size he had last time Christian had seen him. He'd lost maybe fifty pounds, and it seemed like he had shrunk vertically as well. His hair had all but fallen out, and his famous white beard was thin and scraggly. Christian was so shocked that it took him a moment to notice the oxygen tank next his father's chair.

"Dad?"

"So you do remember who I am," said his father, sucking in breath with an alarming wheeze. "I wasn't sure if you would."

"Of course," Christian stuttered. "I just . . . I didn't realise . . ."

"You would have realised," said Margot, following him into the office and closing the door behind her, "if you'd bothered to keep in touch."

"This is none of your business," Christian said. "You don't need to be here."

"Actually, she does," said his dad. "Margot is the general manager now. She has been for a year, ever since I got sick."

"What do you mean, you're sick?" Christian's heart was thumping. "What's wrong?"

As if replying, the old man started to cough, a rasping, hacking noise that sounded painful. Margot walked around the table and held the oxygen mask to his mouth until it had subsided. Christian was so shocked he felt like his legs were about to give way beneath him, but he didn't sit down. He forced himself to keep standing so that he wouldn't look weak — something his dad had always taught him to do.

Not that his dad was standing now.

"Your father has been getting worse," said Margot while his dad collected his breath. "The doctors say he needs to start taking things easy. He needs to stop working."

"Which is why I brought you here," he growled, his blue eyes as fierce as they had always been. "I'm giving you one last shot."

"One last shot at what?" Christian asked. "I told you, I don't want any part of the business."

"You're happier working in the mud?" his dad shot back. "Building flea-infested toilets?"

Christian nodded, feeling the frustrations rise in him. One of the reasons he'd left for good was because his dad had never made an effort to understand him. Money was the only thing that had ever mattered to Lewis Carroll, but Christian had never seen the attraction. He'd taken after his late mother. She'd always told him you couldn't eat gold. When Christian had witnessed the terrible conditions of the factory workers during a buyer's trip to the Philippines and decided to stay to help them, his dad had seen it as a betrayal of him, the family, the business and everything he believed in. How many arguments just like this had he had with the old man before he left five years ago? And now here they were again, at each other's throats just minutes after meeting.

"I'm happy where I am," he said. "I'm sorry you're not well, Dad. I really am. And I'll do what I can to help. But I've made my choice. This business isn't for me."

"You didn't seem to mind when I was giving you all my money," said his dad.

"That's not fair, and you know it," Christian said. "I helped you turn the store around when it looked like everything was going down the drain. I helped you franchise. I earned that money."

It was true. He'd worked insanely hard for four years to save Carroll's during its darkest days after the recession. It had been his idea to open up new stores across the world — London, Paris, Shanghai — and that's where the real money had come from. Without him, Carroll's would have closed its doors years ago. Not that his dad seemed to remember any of that.

"You came," his dad said. "That shows you're at least willing to hear me out."

"Sure," Christian said. "Whatever you need."

"I need you back here." Christian started to protest, but his dad held up a hand. "Margot's right. I need to take a step back or this is gonna kill me. But I need help. The company is in trouble, son. It's on the edge."

"It looks healthy enough down there," said Christian. "I've never seen it so busy."

"Plenty of people," said the old man, wheezing as he drew in a breath. "But nobody is buying. At least not enough to keep the ship afloat. Something's gone wrong, and I don't know what it is. I need somebody to fix it, somebody I can trust."

"What about Margot?" Christian glanced at her and saw the anger in her expression. She wanted this job, he knew, and as much as he hated the thought of giving her anything, he knew she was a better choice. Besides, the last thing he wanted was to be sucked back into the family business.

"Margot is doing an amazing job," his dad said. "She'll continue to run the company. But I need family. I need a Carroll. And you're the only one I've got."

"I've got my own business, Dad," he said. "FutureWorlds. I've got a life out there. I can't just up and leave it."

"You upped and left this one," the old man said. "Besides, why waste your time on a non-profit venture when you could be more than comfortable here?"

Christian sighed. Trying to argue with his father was a lost cause. The old man was still as sharp as a tack, and just as painful.

"Look, I don't want to argue," said his dad. "I figure we've done enough of that. I just . . . I need you, Christian. I'm old, I'm sick. I don't even know how much time I have left. Do this for me, just for a little while. Take a look at the company from the inside, find out what's going on."

"He doesn't even know the company anymore," said Margot.

"Christian has known this company since the day he was born," said the old man. "But you've been gone so long nobody will remember you. You're in the perfect place to get to the heart of whatever is going on."

Christian sighed. All he wanted to do was climb on a plane and head back to his home in the Philippines. But his dad was sick, *really* sick. This situation was obviously stressful for him, and there was a danger it could seriously hurt him. He wasn't being asked to take the company over or anything, just to investigate. He'd saved Carroll's before — he could do it again.

Besides, Margot was right. You didn't say no to Lewis Carroll.

Reluctantly, he nodded.

"Okay, sure," he said. "I'll stay, and I'll see what I can do. But only for as long as it takes to fix whatever has broken."

Margot muttered something beneath her breath, her eyes as dangerous as a snake's.

"Good," said his dad, slapping the desk with one big hand. "I knew you'd come through for me. I think you should—"

"He needs to start somewhere low," Margot interrupted. "A job's just opened up on the cleaning crew. If he's going to go unseen, I can't think of anywhere better."

"A janitor?" said the old man. "Sure, good idea. You can start tomorrow morning. Eight sharp."

Christian nodded. He knew Margot had only suggested the job to humiliate him, but he'd spent the last five years doing messier jobs than cleaning bathrooms, restocking toilet paper and getting stains out of the carpets. Besides, she had a point. If he was going to observe the company, that was the best position to do it from.

"Sure," he said. "Eight."

"Here's everything we know so far." His dad pushed a manila folder across the table. "Read up on it tonight."

Christian took it, waiting for his father to say something else, something *nice*. He thought, after all this time, that he might at least invite him over for dinner at the family house. But he just picked up his oxygen mask and breathed deeply from it, waving his free hand to dismiss Christian from the room. Margot leaned over the old man, helping him, and Christian watched them for a moment before making his way to the door.

His father was dying. The company was dying. Just what kind of Christmas had he come home to?

CHAPTER 3

MERRY

"Excuse me, miss?"

Merry stirred from her daydream, blinking away visions of Christian, to see the balding, middle-aged man in front of her. He was drenched from head to toe, thanks to the freezing rain outside, and his outstretched hand was trembling with the cold.

"Oh," she said. 'Right, sorry."

She handed him the last of her leaflets and he smiled gratefully.

"Go grab a coffee and a gingerbread cookie," she said. "It will warm you up. And don't forget to buy a raffle ticket for the ball!"

The man walked away and Merry stretched her arms above her head, yawning. She had no idea what the time was, but judging how sore her legs were and how dark it was outside, and how badly she needed to pee, it had to be near the end of her shift. The trouble with Carroll's was that there were no clocks anywhere, and she wasn't allowed to carry her phone on her. Usually somebody came to relieve her, but the shop was so busy tonight they must have got waylaid.

She *really* needed the toilet, so she abandoned her post and made her way through the crowds. For a second, she thought she spotted Christian in the crush — a flash of checked jacket — but she tried not to be too disappointed when she realised it wasn't him. It took her a good few minutes to weave her way across the atrium, as she had to field half a dozen requests for help from irritated customers. By the time she reached the elevators she was ready to burst, and she wished she'd taken the longer route to the staff one — especially when she heard a stern voice call out her name. She hung her head, sighing deeply before turning around.

Mrs Cradley stood there, her foot tapping, her arms folded over her clipboard. "Miss Sinclair, where do you think you are going?"

"To the restroom," she replied, trying not to jiggle. "My shift ended at seven."

"Be that as it may," Mrs Cradley said, glancing at her little gold watch. "You are not to leave your position until you are relieved. Is that clear?"

At this rate, she was going to be relieved all over the shop floor. Merry nodded, praying that the woman wouldn't send her back. She could really do with Christian showing up and telling her boss where to go again.

Mrs Cradley stood there for a moment, almost as if she were enjoying torturing Merry. Then she glanced over at the front of the store — there was somebody else there now — and nodded.

"Very well," she said. "But until you are off the shop floor you are still expected to behave like a member of staff, so please put your hat back on your head."

Merry did as she was told, jabbing the elevator button and waiting for what felt like for ever for it to drop to the first floor. Fortunately, nobody else was waiting, and when the doors closed behind her she took a huge sigh of relief. It had been a long day, and her head was pounding, the jazz version of 'Jingle Bells' not helping. She massaged her temples until the doors opened on the tenth floor. There were still quite a few people up there, crowding around Santa's grotto, and she kept her eyes on the floor as she speed-walked to the staff door at the back.

What's the new code? For the life of her she couldn't remember, and she was just starting to panic when the door opened and there he was. Merry skidded to a halt before she ran right into him, but he was so distracted he barely noticed her. Only after a double take did he break into a smile, but he looked paler than he had before, as if some of the vitality had been sucked right out of him.

"Oh, hi," Merry said. "I didn't realise you worked here."

"I didn't," he said, hovering in the door. "But I do now."

Merry had to stop herself from doing a little jig of happiness. That was fantastic news!

He's engaged, you idiot! her brain said, and the disappointment must have registered on her face because Christian laughed.

"You don't look too happy about it," he said.

"No, it's great.' She beamed at him. "I'm really pleased. I'm just surprised — I didn't have you down as the retail type, that's all."

"I'm not, normally," he said. "But a pay check is a pay check, right?"

"Right! So are you on the store floor?" Merry asked. "Sales? Are you in tomorrow? I can show you the ropes if you like. There's not much to it, just smile and be polite. And, you know, don't headbutt the customers."

He laughed, and Merry would have too if she hadn't been so desperate for the toilet. She squirmed, wishing her bladder was a little bigger so she didn't have to run.

"But seriously," she said, "it's easier when somebody helps you out. My first few days here I was a mess, until one of the girls from Perfume took me under her wing. Her name's Alice, not that you need to know that."

Stop wittering!

24

"That's really kind of you," he said. "But I'm not on the shop floor."

"Marketing?" she asked. "No, management. I guess a guy like you tends to run things. Are you my new boss?" She laughed nervously.

Christian popped his lips, fixing her with those perfect brown eyes. "I'm actually working with the cleaning team."

"You're a *janitor*?" The words exploded from her mouth a little louder than she'd intended. She saw the moment his face fell, and she instantly regretted her tone. "Cool. Really, it's cool. I can't tell you what a sty this place would be without you guys. We'd be wading in our own filth. Cleaners make the world go round, if you ask me. You guys are really . . . cool."

Stop talking! she screamed at herself, mentally buttoning her mouth shut. She'd reached a crisis point — if she didn't excuse herself in the next ten seconds then Christian's first job was going to be mopping up the puddle she was about to make.

"Thanks," he said. "Are you okay?"

"Yeah," she lied. "Sure. I mean, kind of. Look, I'm really sorry, but I have to go."

He stood to one side and she practically ran past him. Brilliant. Just brilliant. That really couldn't have gone any worse. The one guy she wouldn't mind impressing and she was running away from him, all because she'd had one too many mochas on her last break. She stopped, catching the door before it could close. Christian stood there, a puzzled look on his face as she waved goodbye.

She peed and then changed quickly, hurrying out of the store. The cold air hit her cheeks, fresh and sharp after the overheated crush of the shop. She tugged her coat more tightly around herself and set off down Fifth Avenue, her boots tapping against the pavement.

The street was still busy, glittering with Christmas lights, and for the first time all day she felt herself relax. Her shift was over. No more fake smiles, no more dodging grabby customers. Just her, the city and the promise of the best hot chocolate in Manhattan waiting a few blocks away.

She wasn't ready to head back to her apartment yet. The thought of the damp creeping up the walls, the rattling pipes and her roommate's endless, tinny reality shows — or, worse, her endless sex noises blaring through the paper-thin walls — made her slow her steps even more.

She wandered along, her breath misting in front of her, and somewhere between the storefronts and the swirling snowflakes her mind drifted right back to Christian. Merry hugged herself more closely, blaming the chill when really it was heat curling low in her belly. It had been a long time since someone had made her feel that kind of spark. A long time since she'd even wanted to feel it.

She caught her reflection in a shop window — pink-cheeked, grinning like an idiot — and rolled her eyes at herself.

Get a grip, Merry. He's engaged, remember?

Still, for a few more steps, she let herself imagine a different ending to tonight. One where she wasn't walking alone. One where she wasn't heading back to a cold apartment and a roommate with no volume control. One where she could be making her own loud sex noises for a change.

By the time she pushed open the door to the hot-chocolate shop, she barely noticed the blast of heat that hit her. She was already warm from the inside out, running on a day-dream-fuelled glow that not even the winter wind could touch.

26

CHAPTER 4

CHRISTIAN

Christian sat alone in the staff room with the manila folder open on his lap, the company logo embossed in gold on the cover. He hadn't slept since arriving in New York. Jetlag still clung to his bones like a wet coat, but it was the contents of the folder that was weighing him down now.

He flipped through page after page of financials, trying to make sense of what he was seeing. Carroll's used to be an empire, his father's pride and joy, but the numbers told a different story now. Revenue was falling fast, costs were ballooning, and profit margins looked like they were a distant memory. There were strange outflows to consulting firms he'd never heard of, plus a supplier that seemed to be billing double what they used to for basic goods. His father hadn't been exaggerating — the red line was steeper than a ski slope. The business was in serious trouble.

As he stared at the numbers, trying to focus, his mind kept slipping sideways. Back to the girl in the Santa hat. Merry. Christian shook his head and tried again to focus on the spreadsheet in front of him, but the words blurred together. What the hell was wrong with him? He hadn't come here for distractions. He now had a mess to unravel and his family company to save. And yet, Merry's gorgeous face kept floating to the front of his mind, disrupting every attempt to concentrate.

Christian scrubbed a hand over his own face. The room felt like it was shrinking and every breath he took reminded him he was back in the city he'd run from. He leaned back in the rickety staff chair and sighed. What he needed was clarity. Or coffee. Or possibly a brain transplant.

Instead, he pulled out his phone and opened the APEX group chat, the only place on earth where he could admit defeat without being judged.

The APEX Club had started as a business incubator, a think tank for billionaires who didn't quite fit the mould. Over the years, the people at its core had become something more. They were friends and battle-tested survivors of deals, disasters and the kind of heartbreak that money couldn't fix. The WhatsApp group had long since evolved into a lifeline and occasional outlet to troll one another.

Christian: *You'll never guess where I am.*

There was a pause. Then, like clockwork, the flood of replies began.

Devlin: *Don't tell us it's another silent retreat. Last time we had to send Nate to break you out.*

Nate: *Hey, they made me do tai chi with goats, it wasn't all bad.*

Rhuairidh: *If this is like the time you "accidentally" ended up on a cruise for pensioners again, just say so. Unless it's a cruise for swingers this time, in which case I also want photographic proof.*

Christian: *Worse. Carroll's Department Store.*

Devlin: *No.*

Blake: *Is this a cry for help?*

Rhuairidh: *Blink twice if you're being held hostage in Menswear.*

Christian: *Dad's ill. He called me back — there's something going on with the store and the business is sinking. So now, I'm undercover as a janitor to try and figure out what's happening.*

Devlin: *Jeez, sorry to hear that, man.*

Nate: *Yeah, that sucks. Sending love, and by love, I mean inappropriate memes and unsolicited business advice, obviously.*

Blake: *That's rough. If you need anything, Dev's your guy.*

Rhuairidh: *Tell your dad we're rooting for him. Also tell him his 1992 Christmas ad still haunts my dreams. Those animatronic reindeer were evil reincarnated.*

Devlin: *Hang in there, mate. And if you do crack the case steal us all novelty socks from Menswear. Size 12, preferably with penguins.*

Blake: *Size 12, who are you kidding? You're not that well-endowed.*

Christian laughed quietly, the tension in his chest easing just enough. Maybe they were idiots, but they were his idiots. He slipped the phone back into his pocket, grabbed the manila folder and stood. He needed to get out of Carroll's and go for a walk to clear his head.

Shoving the folder into his satchel, he slipped down a side corridor most of the current staff probably didn't even know existed. The overhead lights flickered above him as he found what he was looking for — the old freight elevator. It looked just as ancient and unloved as he remembered, coated in dust and humming faintly.

He hauled the door open and stepped inside, pressing the button for the ground floor. The elevator groaned like it was a living thing. It rocked, dust pouring from the ceiling, then it lurched down so hard that he had to grab the side rail to stay upright. The cabin shuddered, gears screeching like they were protesting after years of disuse. For a second, he thought it might stop altogether.

But then it seemed to remember what it was supposed to be doing, clattering down with a noise like a steam train. He let out a slow breath, eyes fixed on the door in front of him, the rhythmic rattle of the descent oddly soothing. It was like the building was reminding him of its age, of how much had changed since he was last here, and how much hadn't.

The elevator came to a juddering stop and he pulled the door open, stepping out into the quiet, empty corridor that ran beneath the store. He took the fire exit at the end and was promptly hit by a blast of icy air.

"Jesus," he muttered, hugging his coat tightly. After months in the Philippines, the New York winter hit like a punch.

He ducked his head against the biting wind and started walking, his boots splashing on the wet pavement. For a few minutes he kept his head down, focusing on keeping warm, but gradually the familiar sights and sounds of the city began to seep into his bones. Despite everything, New York still had its magic.

Everywhere he looked there were signs of Christmas. The city was glowing with it. He passed street vendors selling roasted chestnuts, the smell of them throwing him right back to his childhood. Kids in bright hats skated on a pop-up ice rink. And for the first time in what felt like days, Christian allowed himself to breathe.

He used to love New York at Christmas. As a kid, he would press his nose to the windows at Carroll's, mesmerised by the elaborate displays his father insisted on every year. There had been carriage rides through Central Park, trips to Rockefeller Center to see the tree, late-night hot chocolates from tiny corner cafés. It had felt magical back then. Like anything was possible.

Somewhere along the way, he'd lost that feeling. Buried it under long-haul flights, late-night meetings and an endless hunger to prove himself outside of the family business. He hadn't realised how much he'd missed it until now.

Christian paused on the corner, his breath misting in the freezing air. Maybe he couldn't fix everything tonight. Maybe he couldn't figure out what was happening inside Carroll's yet, but he could do one thing.

He could find a little of that magic again.

Smiling to himself, he turned off Fifth Avenue and on to a street he hadn't walked down in years, drawn by muscle memory alone. There was a tiny shop tucked away on West 43rd — a place that had once served the best hot chocolate he'd ever tasted. His dad used to bring him there after long days at the store, a quiet reward just for the two of them.

It probably wasn't even still there. It had been a small place back then, its windows permanently fogged up and its door jangling every time someone entered. But Christian had a sudden, stubborn urge to try and find it and treat himself to a hot chocolate. A little warmth. Maybe, if he was lucky, a little reminder of who he used to be.

He shoved his hands into his pockets and headed towards it, the cold biting into his skin but a strange sense of hope kindling in his chest.

The little café was still there, squeezed between a jeweller's and a bookstore, its window glowing with soft, golden light. The same faded awning. The same crooked sign swinging in the wind. A rush of nostalgia hit him square in the chest.

He pushed open the door, the bell jangling just as it always had, and the aroma of rich, melted chocolate wrapped around him. The warmth inside was immediate, almost over-whelming after the icy street. And that's when he saw her. Merry. What a coincidence! Of all the places in all the city, she had ended up here too.

She was curled up at a corner table by the fogged-up window, cupping a giant take-out mug between both hands as if trying to absorb its heat. Her cheeks were pink and her red hair was tumbling out from under her knitted hat. She looked small, a little blue around the edges, shivering even in the warm room. Christian's heart did a ridiculous little flip.

Before he could gather himself, Merry dipped one fin-ger into the mountain of whipped cream piled on top of her drink, absently swirling it, then licked it off with a quick flick of her tongue. Something low and dangerous shifted in Christian's gut.

He dragged his gaze away, barely managing to get his brain back online. She hadn't seen him yet. She looked lost in her own world, staring out the window at the snow beginning to fall, a small furrow between her brows as if the weight of the day was pressing down on her.

CHAPTER 5

MERRY

Merry wrapped her hands around the hot chocolate, soaking in its warmth as she sat at a corner table, still shivering from the cold. Her hair dripped steadily on to her shoulders, but she was too tired to care. Why did it always have to be hail and sleet in New York? Where were the fairy-tale drifts of snow that fell on Central Park in the movies?

Fairy tales aren't real, she told herself. *And neither are handsome princes.*

Or are they? She smiled into her cup. She'd met one earlier that evening and she was going to get to work with him too. A stranger who could have stepped straight from the pages of a storybook. Handsome, kind, actually listened when she spoke, hands that could do hard work. She giggled into her drink at the heat creeping up her neck. When she finally looked up, still smiling to herself, a jolt shot through her, just like someone had plucked a string inside her chest.

Christian was standing there like Prince Charming, tall and steady, watching her with eyes the exact rich, warm colour of her hot chocolate.

He lifted a hand in greeting, his mouth tipping into a small smile, and he made a questioning gesture towards her cup, miming a refill. Merry shook her head quickly, hugging her drink closer. She watched as he crossed to the counter to order his own drink, moving with an easy, unhurried confidence that made something inside her spin. She wanted to bottle the moment and keep it for ever. Because somehow, impossibly, his being here felt a little bit like magic.

Christian crossed the café towards her, a smile playing at the corner of his mouth. Merry's gaze caught on it, finding the way his bottom lip was slightly fuller than the top, softer, completely distracting. She dragged her eyes back to his.

"You ordered a hot chocolate too?" Christian said as he reached her table. "You obviously have great taste."

"I would have put you down as a scotch guy," she said, hoping he didn't hear the scratch in her voice.

"Sometimes," he replied. "But on a day like today, and this close to Christmas, nothing beats a bit of liquid heaven."

"Amen to that," Merry said. She brushed a strand of hair away from her eyes, trying to ignore the drumming beat of her heart behind her ribs.

He nodded towards the empty chair across from her. "Mind if I join you while I wait?"

"Not at all," she said, a little too quickly, and his smile deepened into two of the cutest dimples she'd ever laid eyes on.

"So, you come here a lot?" he asked, chuckling to himself at the awful chat-up line.

"Sometimes." She smiled. "It's close, and the staff are nice, and the hot chocolates are the nicest I've ever tasted."

As if on cue the waitress returned, placing a steaming mug on the table in front of Christian.

"Here's one for your man, too," she said, flashing a smile at Merry.

"Oh, he's not my—" Merry started, then she caught sight of Christian shrugging off his lumberjack coat and her insides turned to heat. Somehow, he looked even hotter in a sweater.

Even the waitress had fallen silent at the way his biceps moved through the fabric.

Christian, oblivious to the effect he was having, took a long sip of his drink and sighed deeply, licking the cream from his top lip in a way that made Merry want to jump over the table and help him. The waitress took her leave with a flustered shake of her hands and Merry took a sip of her drink to spare her some time.

"Oh, boy," Christian said, as he licked the spoon from the mug clean. "I have missed these."

"You've been away?" Merry squeaked.

"Yeah, for a while now," he replied. "Nearly five years, to be exact. In Southeast Asia, mainly the Philippines."

"Oh, wow," said Merry. "That's amazing. Don't they have hot chocolate over there?"

"Not like this," he replied, taking a sip. "You get some amazing coffee. I've practically survived on Kapeng Barako."

Merry raised an eyebrow.

"It literally translates as 'manly strong coffee'," he said with a laugh. "But hey, they let me drink it anyway. There's salabat, too, which is crushed ginger and brown sugar in hot water. Tastes like Lysol, if you ask me, but it's great for a bad stomach." He rubbed his stomach, shaking his head. "Which was every day for about a year, until I stopped eating the oxtail stew."

Merry laughed, feeling herself relax a bit more. It had been a long time since a conversation had come this easily. Christian was bright and funny and quick to laugh at himself. Not to mention the kind of gorgeous that made it hard to think straight. Did he have no flaws?

"What were you doing over there?" she asked, just so that he wouldn't think she was staring absently at him.

He opened his mouth to answer, then paused. "This and that," he said, and the way he looked to the side, rather than meet her eye, set off an alarm bell. Had he been doing something bad out there? Maybe even something illegal?

That's the flaw, she told herself. *He's been in prison, and now he's on the run, hunted by crime lords from Asia.*

Christian cleared his throat. "Mostly the same as here — kind of keeping stuff clean, building work, odds and ends, you know."

"Like a caretaker?" she asked, genuinely curious and slightly relieved. "What took you over there in the first place?"

He took another sip of his drink, licking cream off his lip. Merry absentmindedly licked hers, too, drawing her bottom lip between her teeth, her heart fluttering up into her neck.

"I'm sorry," she said, catching his eye and feeling him draw her in. "I ask too many questions."

"No, not at all." His gaze darkened. "It's just been a while since I've sat down face to face with . . . with anyone, really. It was a lonely life over there, nothing but work. To be honest, I moved out so long ago I can barely remember. I just wanted to get away, find a space to do my own thing without my family crowding around me and judging my every move. Does that make sense?"

Merry nodded, taking a beat before replying, the hot chocolate finally cool enough for her to take a sip. "It's why I ended up in New York, all alone. I'm from Nebraska originally."

"Lincoln?"

"Omaha," she said. "My folks are still out there looking after my sister. We get on fine, but there just wasn't enough there to keep me excited. I moved here three years ago after I left university — the *local* university, I should add. Now there's loads to keep me entertained, but I can't afford to do any of it."

"That's New York for you," he said. "How long have you been at Carroll's?"

"Just a few months," she replied. "I was looking for a change. I graduated in media from Nebraska — go Huskers! — and figured I'd get a job out East, but then nothing really happened and I ran out of cash working badly paid newspaper jobs, and here I am. It's an okay place to work, I guess. Most of the people are nice."

36

"Except for that woman," Christian said, playing with his half-empty cup with hands that kept drawing Merry's attention. "The dragon lady."

Merry laughed. "Mrs Cradley, yeah." She shook her head. "She has seriously got it in for me."

"She's just jealous," said Christian.

"Oh, pffft." Merry waved his words away, her heart beating faster.

"Oh, come on," he said. "She's seen how hot you look in a Santa hat. Not everyone could pull that off."

Merry's cheeks exploded, and so did Christian's, turning a wicked shade of Christmas robin red. He twisted his fingers around his cup and Merry wished she could swap places with it.

"Uh . . ." His brows furrowed. "Sorry, that probably came out more intense than I meant it to."

"It's really okay," she replied, croakily. "It's been a long time since anybody called me hot. I didn't dislike it, though."

She really didn't dislike it. And if Christian fancied telling her she was hot on repeat then it wasn't something she would ever get tired of hearing. He looked at her, studying her, and although his mouth opened again, showing off his perfectly imperfect front teeth, nothing came out. Merry gave him a quick grin as the waitress appeared.

"Can I get you folks anything else?" she asked, winking at Merry. "Or are you both heading home?"

I wish, Merry almost said. She shook her head, and so did Christian, and the woman retreated with a knowing smile.

Merry reached for the last of her drink, the warmth of the cup radiating through her fingers. The last thing she'd expected when she'd peeled her frozen backside from her window this morning, was to think about going home with someone tonight. But the way Christian had landed in her lap three times in one day was addictive.

"So," he said, "apart from Mrs Cradley, the staff are okay, yeah? What about the management, the ones right at the top?"

"At the top?" Merry asked, glad of the change of direction. "There are only two people in head office. Lewis Carroll is . . . Well, he seems okay. He's pretty much Santa Claus, right? But he's mostly in the office. Pops down to the shop floor to say hi regularly, though." She frowned. "Actually, I haven't seen him at all recently, now that I think about it, which is unusual. Most of the jobs he used to do are carried out by Margot Miller. She's the other person in the head office and she's pretty much running the place now. You'll meet her. She's nice, so long as you do what you're told."

Christian nodded, his eyes clouding over. It took him a moment to look at her again.

"This is probably a weird question," he asked. "But have you noticed anything odd about the store, anything out of place? Recently, this is."

That was a weird question, Merry thought.

She shook her head. "Odd in what way?"

"Just somebody told me something was going wrong at Carroll's," he said, waving the question away. "Warned me about taking a job there in case the company suddenly went under. I just wondered if you'd noticed anything."

"No," she said, suddenly worried about her own job. "It's been busy, *really* busy, like people queuing to get in the door busy. Everything seems okay. But I've only really known the Christmas rush, remember, fellow newbie."

"Okay, good." Christian said. "I'm glad."

He took a deep sip of his hot chocolate, smiling at her over his cup. It hit her low and deep, sending a pulse of heat straight to her core. God, she wanted to take him home, but she knew herself too well. A one-night stand with a new colleague, no matter how good his hands looked wrapped around his cup, was a disaster waiting to happen.

So she pushed back her chair, gave him a smile that she hoped didn't look as hungry as it felt, and stood up.

CHAPTER 6

CHRISTIAN

"Wait," he said, standing so quickly his chair screeched against the tile floor.

Merry paused, one hand still on the back of her chair, her brows lifted in surprise.

He almost lost his nerve. The soft, wide-eyed look she gave him did something to his chest.

"I just . . ." He glanced down, searching for something that would make sense, something that wouldn't sound like he was desperate to keep her there. Even if he kind of was. "You look cold. Your coat isn't warm enough."

Her mouth opened. Then closed. She glanced down at her duffle like she'd only just remembered it was still soaked through. And her jeans looked frozen stiff with the damp cold. He didn't know how she'd even made it to the café like that, let alone how she was planning to get home.

"You'll freeze," he added, more quietly now.

She looked up again, eyes locking on his with a wicked little glint. "You just said I was hot," she teased.

Christian blinked. Then he barked out a laugh, one hand going to his chest like she'd actually hit him there.

"God, you're trouble," he said, shaking his head and pulling his lumberjack coat from the back of his chair. "Here, wear it. I insist."

She slid her arms into the sleeves and the coat swallowed her whole, hanging off her frame like a blanket with legs.

"I look ridiculous," she murmured, tugging the sleeves over her hands.

"You look warm," he said. "And kind of like a Christmas burrito."

That earned a soft laugh, which made every bit of him light up. Her cheeks were pink again, this time from heat and not from frostbite, and she tilted her head at him like she wasn't quite sure what to make of him.

"You heading home?" he asked.

She nodded. "Yeah. I've gotta go get the train."

"I'll walk with you," he said. "I'm not letting you get sleet-stabbed on my watch."

She raised a brow. "Sleet-stabbed?"

"It's a thing," he said. "It's when the wind turns against you and starts hurling frozen knives at your face. Happens a lot here."

"That sounds . . . charming. And you're going to protect me from that how, exactly?"

"Using my body." He pulled open the café door.

They stepped out into the night and the air hit him like a slap. Sharp and damp and mean. Merry shivered beside him, curling tightly into his coat.

"Okay, you win," she said. "I would have died in just my duffle."

It was only a short walk to the station, but it felt like they were hiking across Antarctica. Christian watched as Merry pulled his jacket closely around her. He shivered violently now that he was outside in this weather wearing nothing but a sweater. A very wet, very clingy sweater.

More than once he caught Merry glancing over at him, her eyes falling on the way his sweater was shrink-wrapped around his body.

"You're going to freeze," she said.

"I haven't got far to go," he replied casually, like the icy wind wasn't slicing straight through him. He didn't add that 'not far' meant a suite at the Plaza on Fifth Avenue. He couldn't tell her that without giving away more than one secret.

Still, she was biting her lip now, staring at the way his soaked top clung to his skin, and he didn't miss the heat in her gaze.

A block ahead, she pointed suddenly. "Come on."

Christian followed her into a narrow discount menswear store, the bell above the door jingling wildly. Warmth enveloped them, thick and dry and filled with the scent of new fabric and leather.

Merry shook the rain out of her hair, scanning the displays. "You need something warmer to wear, stat."

"I'm fine," he said, voice rough.

She ignored him, grabbing a rack of thick, plain zip-up sweaters near the register and holding up a green one to his chest. Her fingers brushed against him and Christian felt desire ripple under his skin.

He froze, breath caught in his throat as her knuckles grazed the wet fabric clinging to his body. His thin jumper was plastered to him, rain-slicked and sort of translucent, doing nothing to hide the fact that he was more than a little built. She looked up at him then, meeting his gaze, and there was something in her eyes that turned his blood to heat.

"I'll try it," he said, his voice coming out hoarser than he'd intended. He reached for the sweater, and when their hands met again it was like his whole body keyed up.

He hadn't been touched in months. He'd been too busy working, too lost in the rhythm of building and fixing and helping others. The connection, that slow, crackling voltage, had sneaked up on him. And now that it was here, he didn't want to let go.

"I'll be right back," he said, already backing towards the changing room as she watched him go.

41

He stepped into the cramped cubicle and closed the curtain, the overhead light buzzing faintly above him. His jumper was drenched and stuck to his skin. He peeled it off slowly so as not to damage the zip-up, shivering slightly at the sudden temperature shift. The mirror in front of him was a bit too close for his liking, but he wasn't mad at what he saw. Water glistened on his skin, his abs contracting instinctively as he pulled the sweater over his arms. But he didn't move to zip it up yet.

He stood there, bare-chested, water still trickling down his pecs, trying to breathe through the heat that was pooling low in his stomach. All because a woman had touched him through his clothes and looked at him like she wouldn't mind doing it again. It was ridiculous.

"Get a grip, Christian," he whispered at himself.

The curtain whipped aside.

"Sorry, what did you—" Merry froze, words dying in her throat as her eyes landed squarely on his bare chest.

Christian stood rooted to the spot, his abs on full display through the unzipped sweater, rain still tracing lazy paths down his torso. For a moment, neither of them moved. The air between them crackled.

Her gaze dragged down his chest, stalled somewhere around his stomach, then snapped back up like she'd just remembered he had a face that she was supposed to be looking at.

"Oops," she said, voice a little too high. "I thought you were talking to me. Sorry. Kind of."

"I wasn't." Heat crept up his neck. "But, uh, I'm not mad about the misunderstanding."

"Neither am I," she murmured, still staring, not even bothering to hide it now. "Jeez, Louise."

Christian let out a soft laugh that hummed low in his chest. "Enjoying the view?"

Her gaze snapped back up again. This time she looked mortified.

"I . . . no . . . I mean, yes . . . but not . . . Oh my God, I'm going to turn around now."

"You don't have to," he said, grinning, finally zipping the sweater the rest of the way. "I'm decent now."

Merry turned away anyway, pressing a hand to her flaming cheek as she muttered, "I'm never going to recover from this. Please don't tell your fiancée about this. I'd hate for them to get the wrong idea."

The grin that spread across Christian's face could've lit up the entire city block. "Oh, I don't actually have a fiancée. I only said that to get Dragon Lady off your back." He pulled the tag from the jumper and stepped out of the cubicle, standing beside her like nothing had happened, even though the space between them felt electric.

"Better?" she asked, letting a slow grin spread across her face and whipping the tag from his hands. "My treat."

"It's fine," he replied. "Honestly."

"There's no way I'm going to let you freeze to death because I stole your jacket," she said, pulling out her purse.

"I'll get it," he said, but she waved him away, handing the money to the cashier.

"It's my fault you're soaked through," she said. "Do you want a jacket too?"

"I'm good." He opened the door to the elements. "Thanks for the present. It feels like Christmas already."

"If all Santa brings you is a twelve-dollar sweater, then I feel sorry for you," she said. "Right, my stop is just down there."

She pointed towards the glowing entrance of the subway station, the light catching in her damp hair as she pulled Christian's coat more tightly around herself.

"Thanks again," she added, lifting a hand in farewell. "For the company. And, you know, for not letting me freeze to death."

Before he could say anything else, she turned and jogged down the steps into the station, her shoes splashing through the puddles. Christian stood there a second too long, the door half-open behind him, cold wind slicing in until the cashier shouted at him to get the hell out and shut the door behind him.

He stepped outside, tucking his hands into the pockets of his new sweater, and started walking north up Fifth Avenue. The streets shimmered with rain and twinkling reflections, taxis crawling by in ribbons of yellow. He barely noticed the rain anymore, lost in his thoughts about the drink he'd just had and the girl he'd got to know.

He reached his hotel and stepped through the revolving doors, the doorman nodding politely. Inside the elevator, he caught his reflection in the gold trim. The green sweater clung to his shoulders. He pressed the button for the top floor and leaned against the back wall, his thoughts far from the luxury suite waiting upstairs.

He'd almost told her what he was doing back in New York. The words had been there, perched on the edge of his tongue. But it was too risky, because he didn't really know her well enough yet. He wanted to know more.

He wanted to know what kind of music she listened to when she was alone. Whether she hated mornings or was the type to bounce out of bed with the sunrise. What made her eyes do that sparkly thing they'd done in the changing room. If he could make her laugh like that again, but on purpose this time — that wouldn't be a chore.

The elevator chimed and the doors slid open. Christian stepped out into the plush hallway and made his way to his room. He unlocked the door, stepped inside and let it close behind him with a soft click. Then he pulled off the sweater, held it in his hands for a long moment and hung it carefully over the back of a chair.

Just in case he needed it again tomorrow.

CHAPTER 7

MERRY

Merry flew through the door of Carroll's so fast she almost collided with the greeter who was standing there.

"I'm sorry!" she yelled, smearing the rain from her face so that her blurry eyes could focus. The fierce wind snatched at the lumberjack coat, threatening to pull her back on to Fifth Avenue, but she stood her ground, her teeth chattering against the cold.

"Welcome to Carroll's!" the greeter said. "Have a merry— Oh, Merry!"

Merry squinted, recognising her friend Alice.

"Sorry, Alice," she said. "I'm late."

"*So* late," Alice said, checking her watch. "Like, thirty minutes. Again. What happened this time?"

"Traffic," she replied, running past Alice and heading for the elevators. Mrs Cradley would be stalking the ground floor with her clipboard, and Merry prayed that she wouldn't see her. She couldn't stand the idea of being told off again by the Dragon Lady.

This time, she couldn't fight the smile. Christian had given Mrs Cradley that nickname last night and she'd thought about little else since. Christian that was, not Mrs Cradley. She wanted to try and stalk him on social media now she knew he was single, but she had no idea what his surname was. So instead, Merry had gone over their conversation as she'd fallen asleep. The sight of him in the changing room was for ever burned into her mind, and not even her roommate's noises had dampened her spirits. In fact, quite the opposite. She'd had to put on her headphones and listen to calming brown noise to stop herself getting too worked up to sleep. Turned out her headphones also blocked out her alarm, and she'd slept in, again.

Christian had mentioned his work in Asia. He'd spoken a little about his early life, too, right here in New York, but they had obviously been less happy times because his eyes had gone dark and his smile had ghosted away. She wondered why, if things were so bad here and so good overseas, he had come back to New York — especially to work a cleaner's job at a department store. But that was one thing he hadn't spoken about, and she hadn't asked.

Besides, whatever the reason was, she was happy that he was here.

She kept her eye out for him as she crossed the floor, weaving in and out of the crowds and while waiting for the elevator. But there was no sign. She sniffed at the collar of his jacket and smiled into the thick wool.

Entering the elevator with a group of smartly dressed older gentlemen, she rode to the top floor and darted to the staff door, fumbling in the code. Fortunately, Mrs Cradley wasn't there, and neither were the other managers. Checking the roster and seeing that she was in Jewellery, she changed into her uniform and Santa hat, then made her way to the third floor. There were already two dozen customers there, and a very flustered Diane was fighting the queue. She caught sight of Merry and waved.

"I'm so sorry," Merry said as she slipped behind the counter. "I'm so late!"

"Duh, *really*?" Diane said. "It had better be because of a tall, dark stranger or I'm going to be very annoyed."

Merry laughed, a little more awkwardly than she'd intended.

"Um . . ." she said. "Traffic?"

"Yeah, right," Diane said. "But don't worry. I covered for you. Told the old bat you were taking a customer to the electronics department after making a killer sale."

"*Thank you*," Merry mouthed, before turning to the next customer in the line. "Hey! How can I help?"

It was a kid who couldn't have been older than eighteen, and he nervously told her he was looking for something special for his long-time girlfriend who was about to leave for university in California. Merry smiled, chatting to him as they made their way between the cabinets. Most of the jewellery in Carroll's was way too expensive for him, his eyes just about popping out of his head as he stared at the diamonds and rubies and pearls on display. But there were some more affordable items and Merry let him take his time. After a few minutes he was confidently telling her about his girlfriend, and about how he wanted to do something to make her feel special — even though he worried about her being so far away from him.

"That's really sweet," she said, handing him a slim chain with a silver pendant in the shape of a spiral. "You're so lucky, and so is she. I've always liked this piece. There's something about spirals that's . . . reassuring, I guess. Love isn't always straightforward, there are ups and downs, and countless bends. Trust me, I know. But with a spiral, even though you don't always travel in a straight line, even though the journey can weave in and out of good times, you're always moving forward."

He nodded, smiling.

"And it's only a hundred ninety-nine dollars," she said. "You'll still have fifty left for a bunch of flowers."

"That's great!" he said. "I'll take it!"

She walked him back to the sales desk and rang it through, placing it in a display box and wrapping it as delicately as she was able.

"There should be a charge for the box, but I'll comp it," she said, handing it to him. "Just don't tell anyone!"

"Thank you!" he said, grinning.

"Just remember, it will be hard, but you can get through it," she said. "All you have to do on the bad days is remember the good ones, okay?"

"Sure," he said. "And really, thank you."

"Have a great day," she said, watching him walk away. "Merry Christmas!"

She smiled to herself, wondering if all the day's customers would be as charming and sweet as the kid had been. She leaned against the counter, letting herself exhale for the first time since she'd stepped through the doors. The warmth of the store had finally started to seep into her bones, and the smile from that sweet customer lingered. Maybe today wouldn't be a complete disaster after all.

She glanced over at Diane, who was deep in conversation with a woman debating between two charm bracelets. With the queue temporarily under control, Merry allowed herself a moment to people-watch and then immediately regretted it.

Across the department, just behind the crystal tree display, stood Mrs Cradley and Margot Miller, their heads bent close together in a way that could only mean one thing — trouble. Mrs Cradley's clipboard was tucked under one arm and her free hand gestured sharply at something on a folded sheet of paper while Margot nodded solemnly, her mouth twisted in that tight, judgemental way she always wore when she was about to report someone for dress-code violations or loitering in the stock room.

Merry quickly looked down, straightening her Santa hat. Was it her they were talking about? Maybe they'd found out she'd been late again. Maybe Diane's clever cover story hadn't worked. Or maybe it had nothing to do with her. Maybe they were plotting something else entirely, some new rota rearrangement or another holiday-hours reshuffle that would ruin everyone's plans.

Still, the sight of them whispering filled her with dread. Nothing good would ever come from Mrs Cradley and Margot Miller joining forces.

Before she could dwell on it too long, a shadow loomed in front of her counter.

"Excuse me," a brusque voice snapped. "Is *anyone* going to help us?"

Merry blinked up at the man who had appeared in front of the case, tall and square-shouldered in an expensive-looking wool coat. His salt-and-pepper hair was slicked back and his lips were twisted into a look of long-suffering impatience. Beside him, his wife, she assumed, stood with her arms folded, eyes already scanning the jewellery with a mouth like a cat's bum.

"I'm so sorry for the wait," Merry said brightly. "How can I help today?"

"We're looking for a necklace," the woman cut in, her voice sharp and nasal.

Merry stepped in front of the first counter, but the woman scowled at her.

"Be better, do we look like people who shop in the mass-produced section? These are lab-created diamonds." She waved a dismissive manicured hand. "If I wanted something fake, I'd go to Macy's."

Merry's smile faltered. "Of course," she said, guiding them to the fine jewellery case. "If you're looking for something special, we've just had a new collection arrive."

She opened the cabinet and carefully laid out a velvet tray of necklaces. "These are all certified stones, and many are unique to Carroll's this season."

The woman leaned in, peering closely. "That one's tiny," she sniffed, pointing at a delicate teardrop diamond. "And

49

that setting looks cheap. Honestly, I don't know what's happened to this place."

Merry felt her shoulders sink and she looked to the next section for inspiration.

"If I may suggest—"

The man interrupted her before she could finish her pitch. "We don't need suggestions from a wet-haired sales assistant with a wrinkled hat and smudged makeup."

Heat flooded Merry's cheeks. She wanted to snap back and tell them she was doing her best, but she bit her tongue. Diane caught her eye and gave her a sympathetic wince as she focused back on the tray. In front of her, the couple kept complaining, voices carrying through the crowd.

"Honestly, Harold, I don't know why you insisted we come here. The standards are slipping. My mother used to shop here when class meant something."

She'd known it was too good to last. Fairy tales didn't survive daylight in real life. Not for girls like her.

She took a breath and squared her shoulders, bracing herself for her bump back down to earth.

CHAPTER 8

CHRISTIAN

It really wasn't too bad at all if you didn't mind the stickiness.

Christian dipped his mop into the bucket and ran it along the bathroom floor. Somebody had spilled what had to be three gallons of strawberry milkshake by the sinks, and it had stuck to the tiles like glue. But it was coming away easily enough, and there was almost something therapeutic about the work, the rhythm of the mop and the meditative quiet.

Besides, Christian had worked on much dirtier jobs. Once, when he'd been building his first school in Rapu-Rapu, he'd pickaxed the main sewer pipe, the geyser of filthy water soaking him from head to toe. It had taken him and two more guys the better part of an hour to seal it, and the smell hadn't washed away for a week. Back then, he'd just set up FutureWorlds, and he had plenty of staff who could have taken over the physical jobs, but Christian liked getting his hands dirty. Well, maybe not as dirty as that, but he liked to be the one out there with a hammer and tacks, or a saw, or a paintbrush. There was something amazing about being able to create a school with your own hands and not just pay for

51

it. Even when you ended up covered in filth — even when you were drenched in sweat and blood and mud. It was almost spiritual.

That's what his dad had never understood. Lewis Carroll had inherited the store from his own father, Cornelius. Although he'd transformed the little shop into the behemoth it was today, Lewis had never really had to build anything from scratch. He'd always sat behind his desk and given the orders, like a general. He'd never had to go on the buyers' trips to Africa, to Asia. He'd never seen the workhouses and the mines that created the beautiful fabrics and jewellery and gadgets that filled his store.

Christian preferred to be a soldier. He'd never forgotten his first trip to the Philippines, to the cramped and noisy factory that supplied the bedsheets and duvet covers for Carroll's. After that day he'd vowed to dedicate himself to helping others, rather than simply adding more wealth to his own pockets, or those of his father.

So what are you doing here? he asked himself.

He squeezed the mess out into the bucket and ran the mop along the last stretch of floor. He wasn't going to be here for ever. Until New Year, maybe, then he'd fly home. The honest truth was he should have said no to his dad straight away, but seeing the old man so frail, so ill, had been shocking. As ruthless as Lewis was, he was still Christian's father, and amid all the bad memories of his childhood were a few sparkling, wonderful ones — occasions when his dad had taken the afternoon off and whisked him to the zoo in Central Park, or the library. There had even been Christmases where his dad had given Christian the best present of all: his time.

The least he could do was see this through and be there for his dad when he needed him.

Christian stuck the mop back in the bucket and washed his hands — hands that were already rough and scarred from years of hard work. He dried them on his blue overalls, glancing at his reflection in the mirror.

There was another reason he was glad to have stayed, and that reason had kept him awake all night — not Merry personally, he was sad to say, but *thoughts* of her, *dreams* of her, gallivanting through his mind until the early hours of the morning. *Man, the dreams.* It was so unexpected, mainly because he hadn't been looking for anyone at all. He'd had a couple of dates overseas, but never a relationship, because nothing was as important as the work and there was simply no time to fall in love.

He scrubbed harder at the taps, trying to push the image of her from his mind. Maybe taking a break from FutureWorlds and coming home had given him the chance to breathe, to rest. Maybe that's all it was — a momentary breath in the chaos.

But still, he couldn't stop thinking about the way she'd looked at him in that changing room and the way he'd wanted her to give in to whatever the voice in her head was telling her to do.

Those green eyes, dangerous in their sparkle, like they could see through him and still want to linger. Her cheeks were always rosy, freckled like something out of a dream, and her mouth lit him up in places he was trying very hard to ignore right now. Even just thinking about it made his pulse thrum and his overalls feel snug.

It wasn't lost on him how tempting it would be to lean into his feelings. He'd caught himself more than once wondering what it would be like if the store was shut for the night, just the two of them locked in, him kissing her breathless beside the fake tree and baubles. Maybe more than just kissing. Maybe a hell of a lot more.

But he couldn't go there. Not when he was keeping secrets and when he'd be gone by January. Merry deserved more than a holiday fling with a guy passing through, so he was keeping his thoughts on a short leash. Or, at least, he was trying to.

The restroom door opened, making Christian jump and empty of all his thoughts into the bucket. A well-dressed older man walked in, looking at Christian like he was a rat that had scurried out of the toilet.

"Careful, sir," Christian said. "The floor is a little wet."

The man ignored him, marching into a cubicle. Christian put the bucket back on to his janitor's trolley and wheeled it outside. The store was heaving, even though it wasn't even ten yet. He politely weaved his way between the groups of customers, but nobody looked at him. He was invisible in his janitor's overalls, and as much as he hated Margot, he knew she had been right — this was the perfect role for him to investigate what was happening in the store. He'd spoken to several other members of the janitorial team already and they had all agreed that something strange was going on. For a start, three of the team had been laid off in the last month, as well as quite a few other people from different departments. The store was chronically understaffed, and customers were starting to notice. Nobody knew why it was happening, though.

He was just entering the aisles of the kitchen department when he heard his radio bleep. He unclipped it from his belt, hearing a short hiss of static then the gruff Brooklyn accent of Harvey, the senior janitor.

"Anyone on three?"

"I'm on four," Christian said. "What's up?"

"Spillage in the watch department," Harvey said. "They's freakin' out 'cos it's on the Rolexes."

"I'm on it," Christian said. He returned the radio to his belt, wheeled the trolley through the staff doors and down the bleak back corridor to the new freight elevator. It was a short ride down, and when the doors opened he pushed the trolley out on to the third floor. It was even busier there, and it took him an age to get through the mob of customers. It was weird, because there were only three staff members in sight — way too few for such a busy day. They were all flustered, fighting off impatient customers like they were under attack.

It was only as he walked past Jewellery that he recognised Merry. He quickly realised he was grinning like an idiot and forced the smile away before anyone noticed. He turned his attention back to where he was going, before he accidentally wheeled into somebody, but something drew his gaze back to Merry. She looked as stressed as the other members of staff, but there was a desperation to her expression that made him think it was more than just being overworked. She looked worried, her mouth a grim line, her teeth clenched.

Christian stopped walking, studying the people she was talking to. One was a well-built man in his fifties who looked like he was ready to coach a high school football team. The other was a glamorous woman dressed for a wedding — or maybe a funeral. The man had his arm possessively around the woman, holding her like he was worried she was going to run away. But it was the way he was looking at Merry that made Christian feel like his blood was simmering. There was something cruel in his expression. He had the face of a bully.

The Rolexes could wait. Christian edged the stubborn trolley around and walked into the jewellery department, making his way slowly towards where Merry was standing. Nobody paid him any attention, apart from to step warily out of the way of his slopping bucket, and it didn't take him long to cross the room.

". . . though with the way she looks I wouldn't trust her to wrap a sandwich, let alone something expensive," he heard the man say. "Don't they have any standards here anymore?"

"Sorry," Merry replied, a tremor in her voice. She was facing away from Christian, so he edged a little closer, running a cloth over the glass face of a cabinet to wipe away an imaginary mark. "That's fine. A diamond?"

"Obviously," said the man. "A big one. We're not here to mess around with cheap tat. Though by the looks of it, that's all you're selling."

The woman next to him gave a sharp laugh. "Honestly, I've seen better displays at a yard sale. And the staff . . ." She eyed Merry's uniform and freckled face with a sneer. "Well, I guess it's festive if you're going for thrift-store elf."

Christian's hand clenched more tightly around the cloth, wishing it were the man's smug, over-moisturised face. They didn't even know Merry, and yet they were treating her like dirt beneath their designer shoes.

Merry, to her credit, didn't flinch. "We have a range of diamond cuts," she said calmly, pulling open the case behind her. "If you let me know your budget, I'll be happy to show you a few options."

The man gave a smirk. "Oh, we're not worried about budget. I just want something that'll make every woman in the room jealous. Not that you'd know anything about that."

That did it. The only thing Christian wanted to do was punch the man's lights out, but that would only land him and Merry in trouble. Instead, he pulled the stinking mop out of its bucket and walked up to the couple. The floor was immaculately clean, but he slapped the mop down at the man's feet hard enough to splash water all over his brogues and her ridiculous heels.

"Excuse me!" the woman yelled, stepping back so clumsily that she almost fell. "What are you doing?"

"Sorry, lady," Christian said. "Just trying to get rid of a nasty mess."

He flicked the mop over the man's shoes again, and he stumbled away.

"What's your problem, buddy?" the man roared. "You'd better be more careful with that."

Christian glanced at Merry, whose mouth was open in surprise. He winked at her, then swept the mop around again.

"These irritating stains just won't get the message," he said, jerking the mop across the floor, dirty water splashing over their shoes. The man and woman were retreating fast now, other customers moving out of their way with astonished smiles on their faces.

"You're going to pay for this," the man yelled, jabbing a finger at Christian. "I'm going to make sure you never work here again, you hear me? You stupid, good-for-nothing janitor."

Christian flicked the mophead up, a spray of brown water splashing over the man's face. He finally turned around, grabbed his wife by the arm and marched her towards the elevators. Christian waited for the door to close behind them before turning to Merry.

A smile danced over her face, and he almost had time to return it before it vanished and Merry turned and bolted for the staff door.

CHAPTER 9

MERRY

Merry ran into the staff restroom and slammed the door shut behind her. Fortunately, there was nobody else in there, because the tears were pouring out of her, unstoppable. She wasn't even sure why — partly the shock of how the man and his wife had spoken to her, partly the way the woman had looked her up and down, partly the sugar hangover from all that hot chocolate.

But it wasn't just that. It had been the way Christian had ridden to her defence, swinging his mop like a lance. She didn't understand why he'd done that. The man might have hit him — and she'd seen enough angry customers in her time to know how quickly things could escalate. She had no doubt that the couple would go straight to management and report it. Christian was going to lose his job, and there was a good chance she could as well — right before Christmas, too.

She gripped the sink and sobbed, tears falling down her cheeks like raindrops. Why did men have to be so annoying? Why did they always have to do such senseless and hurtful things?

"Hello?"

Merry almost didn't hear the voice over her choked sobs, and she smudged away the tears the best she could.

Go away, go away, go away, she prayed, but then somebody knocked again.

"Merry?" said Christian. "Are you in there?"

"No," she said. "Please leave me alone."

"I'm really sorry," he said, his words muffled by the door. "That was stupid. I never should have done it."

"You shouldn't have." She pulled some paper free from the towel dispenser and wiped her face. She looked even more of a mess than usual, her eyes puffy and her nose as red as her cheeks. Under no circumstances whatsoever could anybody see her like this, especially not Christian. "Please, just go."

"I will," he said. "Just as soon as you tell me you're okay."

"I'm not okay," she shot back. "You had no right to do that."

"I . . . I know," he said. "I just heard what he said, and it drove me crazy. He shouldn't have said those things."

Merry ran the taps and splashed water on her face, recovering a little.

"I know I don't know you, not really," Christian went on from the other side of the door. "But last night was . . . I felt good about it, I felt good about being with you. I just heard him being rude and I wanted to do something to help. I know what I did was the wrong thing, I just had to do something. You looked so . . . sad."

She still looked sad. Merry studied herself in the mirror and sighed. If somebody had told her a few days ago that a handsome, kind stranger would come into her life and scare away mean people with a mop, she would have laughed at them. But that's exactly what he had done. He'd chased those horrid people away with a stinky mop.

To her surprise, a laugh tumbled out of her now. The image of the man and his wife running from Carroll's with wet shoes and mop water on their faces would stay with her for the rest of her life.

Something was rattling outside, and she cocked her head to try to work out what the noise was.

"What are you doing?" she asked when she couldn't figure it out.

"Hanging up an out-of-order sign," Christian replied. "It's a perk of the job. Just take your time. I'll leave you in peace. I really am sorry."

She heard the squeak of his trolley and before she even knew what she was doing, she ran to the door and yanked it open. Christian looked back, pausing.

"Come here," she said. "Let me explain."

He did as she asked, hesitating for a moment at the door.

"This is a ladies' bathroom," he said, glancing over his shoulder. "I shouldn't . . ."

"You're not going to burst into flames," she said. "Besides, you're the janitor — you have to clean everywhere, right?"

"Fair point." He ducked past her and gave her a faint smile.

She let the door close, watching him as he made his way to the sinks and perched on them, running a hand through his dark hair. The light was muted, but a shaft of winter sun spilled in through a window, landing right on him. His eyes were such a rich shade of chestnut brown that they didn't look real, and when he looked at her, waiting patiently for her to speak, a storm of butterflies flew wildly in her stomach.

Merry swallowed hard. "It's me that should be apologising," she said, and when he started to argue she held up a hand. He fell respectfully silent. "It's not just what they were saying, it's the way they were saying it. Like I was stupid and ugly and they deserved a better server than me. I know it shouldn't matter and I should let it wash over me, but it hits hard because I've heard it all before. I grew up with it. 'Ginger freak.' 'Clown mouth.' 'Freckle face.' Kids are cruel to those who are different, and because my sister has cerebral palsy, that makes our whole family different. They thought it gave them free rein to bully me more than they would have done."

Christian didn't interrupt. He just listened, his expression shifting slowly from sympathy to something dangerously protective.

"I've spent years trying to convince myself that it doesn't matter what other people think," she went on. "But sometimes, out of nowhere, it cracks through. Like today."

Christian shook his head and Merry's breath caught as he stepped closer.

"You shouldn't have to fight so hard to feel like you're enough," he said. "Because you are."

Merry took a step towards him. "You don't know that," she whispered.

"I see it."

The silence between them pulsed. She could feel the beat of it in her fingertips and her body leaned in to his without her permission. They were almost close enough to touch, and the quiet room suddenly felt strangely intimate.

Christian fixed his eyes on her, the corner of his mouth twitching into a kind smile. "Thank you for forgiving me," he said, almost in a whisper.

She took another step, every single one of her cells urging her to press her body against his. There was just something magnetic about him, even in his creased overalls, even in the store bathrooms. There was something she couldn't resist.

"Thank you, for standing up for me," she said, lifting her face. "Even though I didn't ask you to. I don't think he'll be back in a hurry."

"If he comes back, he'd better be wearing rubber boots," said Christian, a smile tugging at his mouth.

He lifted a hand as if to stroke her cheek or tuck a loose strand of hair behind her ear, but stopped short, looking at his hand hovering there in the space between them. His chest filled and stuttered and she felt it like a spark. Every inch of her burned with the want of his touch.

Neither of them moved, the air around them electric.

"Christian . . ." Her lips parted.

61

"What on earth is going on in there?"

The voice was like a klaxon, and Merry leaped back in shock. Somebody was pushing the bathroom door open — and only one person had a voice like that.

"Dragon Lady!" Christian hissed. "Hide!"

She didn't hesitate, just threw herself into the nearest cubicle and shut the door behind her. Climbing on to the toilet, she crouched down and listened to the clack of Mrs Cradley's heels as she marched into the room. She could just about see through the crack in the door as Christian pulled a screwdriver from his belt, holding it like a vampire hunter coming face to face with Dracula. Fortunately, Mrs Cradley didn't seem to recognise him from yesterday.

"Excuse me!" she snapped. "What are you doing?"

"Uh . . ." Christian stammered. "I was just asked to fix a toilet."

"Why? What's wrong with it?"

"Uh . . . it . . . exploded?" he said. Despite the tension in the room, Merry had to cover her mouth to stop the laugh escaping.

"Exploded?" Dragon Lady asked.

"Yeah, there was . . . uh . . . *stuff* everywhere. I was trying to repair it."

"Are you a qualified plumber?"

"No, I'm just the janitor."

"Then you will leave this facility immediately and call for the relevant technician. Am I clear?"

"Yes, ma'am," Christian said, glancing at the cubicle where Merry was hiding. "I just need—"

"Now!" barked Mrs Cradley, loud enough for the word to echo off the tiled walls. Christian flinched, walking from the room like a chastised schoolboy. Mrs Cradley looked at the row of cubicles, and for a dreaded moment Merry thought she was coming to investigate. But she pivoted on her heels and exited, plunging the room into silence.

CHAPTER 10

CHRISTIAN

"There you are! Where on earth have you been?"

Christian hurried down the aisle, stopping at a display case full of expensive watches. A mug of milky coffee had been spilled on the top of it, and even though somebody had done their best to wipe it up, droplets were plopping through the cracks. A harassed cashier stood there, a pile of napkins in one hand. A queue had built up, people clamouring for service. Christian pulled his cleaning products from the trolley and excused his way through the crowd.

"I've been waiting for nearly fifteen minutes," the cashier said.

"Sorry," Christian replied. "There was an emergency in the restrooms."

"More important than a $10,000 Rolex full of coffee?" she shot back, her face creased with annoyance.

Christian mumbled another apology, waiting for her to unlock the case. This was something he was discovering all too quickly: that when you were wearing a janitor's overalls, people treated you like you were a servant, like you were trash. It was a good test of character, he thought, seeing how somebody reacted to him when he had a mop in his hands. He'd bet, if this cashier knew he was Christian Carroll, heir to the Carroll empire, she'd have been a lot more polite.

"Come on!" she snapped as he pulled the first watch from its stand and checked it. There was a spot of coffee on the face, but it was otherwise unharmed. It was a Cellini, very similar to one he owned, and it retailed at over $20,000. He carefully wiped the face with a lint-free cloth, then handed it to the woman. He'd always been conscious of the money he had, especially when he'd started to earn his own millions. But now, dressed in a janitor's uniform, it seemed particularly nauseating that a single watch could cost more than he would earn doing this job for a year.

"Excuse me, could you please hurry up?" barked a man behind him.

Christian did his best to smile politely as he cleaned another two Rolexes. One — an Oyster Perpetual — had been quite badly drenched, but they were waterproof so it would be easily remedied. He polished it as best he could, then handed it over. He used half a roll of kitchen paper to mop up the coffee, then a clean cloth to make the glass and floor of the cabinet as good as new. There was something immensely satisfying about the work, but nobody seemed to appreciate it.

"You can go now," said the cashier as the crowd surged forward.

"Sure," he said. "No worries."

He turned to walk away, whispering 'You're welcome' under his breath, then changed his mind. "Hey, why are you on your own here? It's so busy."

"How would I know?" she replied, taking payment from the rude man who had spoken to Christian earlier. "There used to be three of us, but there have been layoffs."

She waved him away like he was an annoying fly. He collected his trolley and squeezed out of the crowd. Only when he was back in the relative quiet of the staff corridor did Christian finally exhale. The fluorescent lights hummed overhead, and the distant din of the shop floor faded into the background. His shoulders ached, his hands smelled like disinfectant, and his pride was still somewhere on the floor back by the Rolexes. But it wasn't the coffee or the cashier or the rude customer that had him rattled. It was Merry.

He raked a hand through his hair and leaned against the wall, the image of her in that cramped bathroom seared into his brain. The curve of her neck when she turned to him. The flash of something dangerous when their eyes had locked.

He'd been an idiot, no question. Charging in like some knight with a mop and a martyr complex, trying to protect her when she hadn't asked for it. But, God, when she'd looked at him in the aftermath, he'd felt something shift. Something had crackled in the charged air between them and he was sure he hadn't been the only one to feel it.

The truth was he wanted her, and he needed to tame the ache in him if he was going to get through the rest of the day. Or the rest of the month. Because no matter how much he wanted to press his mouth to the warm skin of her throat, to learn the scent of her and the sounds she'd make if he ran his hands down her body, it wouldn't be fair. She deserved more than someone who was leaving in a couple of weeks. And until he could figure out how to be honest with her, he had no business thinking about her like that. Even if he couldn't stop.

Christian sighed, pressing the button for the service elevator. He was waiting for it to arrive when his radio hissed again.

"Chris?" said Harvey. "You still on three?"

"Yeah," he replied.

"They need you on ten," he went on. "Out back, head office. No idea what the job is, but they asked for you."

Christian knew exactly what the job was. He rode the elevator to the top floor, pushing the trolley back out through the toy department. Santa Claus was sitting outside the grotto, a young girl on his knee and a line of people waiting to speak to him. Christian squinted at the man, shaking his head in disbelief. It couldn't be the same Santa whose knee he had sat on when he was a kid, could it? It certainly looked like him, but he didn't seem to have aged a day.

As if he could sense that he was being watched, Santa glanced up, a twinkle in his eye as he looked right at Christian. Despite the fact he was nearly thirty years old, Christian grinned and waved.

The smile didn't last long. He used the new code to open the staff door, leaving his trolley in the corridor, and headed past the break room and the locker room to the offices at the back. There was no mess to clean up here, he knew — not in the conventional sense, anyway.

He stopped outside the door to his dad's office, knocking twice.

"What?" came the gruff reply.

Christian opened the door, trying to make sense of the gloom after the blindingly bright corridor. "Dad? You needed to see me?"

"Come in."

He did as he was asked, closing the door behind him. It was only when he turned to face the desk again that he noticed Margot sitting in the armchair in the corner of the room.

She glared at him. "Picking fights now, are we?" she asked. "Attacking customers with a broom? What kind of example are you setting for the rest of the staff?"

Christian sighed. "It was a mop."

"We had to offer to dry clean her dress and shoes," Margot went on. "Money we could have done without sp—"

"Leave it," growled Lewis Carroll. He seemed even older than he had yesterday, slumped over his desk, the oxygen mask hanging around his neck, but his words carried the same power and authority they always had. "They probably had it coming. Right, son?"

"Yes," said Christian. Then, thinking of what Merry had said, "Actually, no. I acted way out of proportion. I'm sorry."

Margot grinned smugly, but his dad waved his words away. "I don't care." He broke into a fit of hacking coughs.

Margot got up to help him, but he waved her away too. He inhaled through the mask, taking a moment to catch his breath. "It's forgotten. Have you learned anything?"

Christian nodded, walking to the chair in front of his father's desk. He sat down, leaning forward with his elbows on his knees. "I'm getting a sense of the place," he said. "There are major queues forming, customers getting angry at the wait and leaving without buying anything. From what I've learned, it's a staffing issue. There just aren't enough people here, especially for this time of year."

"That's rubbish," spat Margot. "My staffing levels are perfect."

"So why the layoffs?" Christian asked. "Why are you letting so many people go?"

"What?" barked his dad. "What layoffs?"

"The janitorial team, the jewellery department, Kitchen, everywhere." He looked at Margot. "This is your doing."

"We haven't made any layoffs," she said, her eyes like daggers. "And if you're going to accuse me of something, you'd better have evidence to back it up."

"Hey, calm it down," said his dad. "Margot, leave us."

She stood up, fuming, opening her mouth to protest, then seemed to think better of it.

"I told you, Lewis," she said as she walked from the room. "He doesn't know the business. He doesn't know the company."

Then she was gone, the door slamming behind her.

Lewis pushed his chair back, struggling to his feet, and Christian ran around the desk to help him.

"I'm okay," the old man said. "I'm not dead yet."

They stood face to face, and Christian was shocked at how small his dad looked — as if somebody had shaved a foot off his height. He was stooped and broken, each breath coming in short, rapid wheezes. All Christian wanted to do was wrap his father in a hug, but years of emotional absence kept him at bay.

"Grab that." Lewis nodded at the oxygen tank.

Christian picked it up, careful not to pinch the tube. His dad collected a walking stick from the side of the desk and shuffled across the room, leading the way into the corridor. There were a few members of staff out there, all of whom nodded to their boss, and all of whom completely ignored the janitor by his side.

"People have really said that?" his dad asked. "That there've been layoffs?"

"Yeah," Christian said. "Too many for it not to be true. You must have a record of employees, of who has joined and who has left?"

"That's Margot's department now. She works with Mrs Cradley on the background stuff."

"And you trust her?" Christian asked.

His dad pressed the buzzer and shouldered through the door into the store. Christian hefted up the oxygen tank, following him out. His dad was breathing hard, and Christian was worried that he might be overdoing it. But it turned out he wasn't going far. He stopped at the edge of the children's department, close enough to see Santa passing a gift to a young boy. Overhead, 'All I Want For Christmas' was playing.

"You recognise him?" his dad asked.

"Santa?" said Christian. "I think so. I couldn't be sure. Is it really the same guy?"

"Of course." There was almost a smile on his dad's face. "I remember putting you on his knee when you were ten months old, holding you there while he asked you what you wanted for Christmas. You know what you did?"

Christian shook his head. It was so unlike his dad to reminisce like this that the question took him by surprise.

"You threw up all over his trousers," he said, coughing out a rumbling laugh. "We had to rush him into the bathroom to clean it off. Luckily the store wasn't open yet, we were just setting up. We had time to dry clean them. But for the rest of that rehearsal, Santa gave out gifts in his jockey shorts."

Christian laughed. "Who is he?"

His dad turned to him, blinking his watery eyes.

"What sort of dumb question is that?" he said after a moment. "He's Santa."

His dad sucked in a breath through his oxygen mask. His eyes were dull and heavy again, his mouth downturned and serious.

"I trust Margot," he said, wiping his lips on the back of his hand. "She's ruthless, and she wants the top job, but I trust her."

Christian still had his doubts, but he kept them locked behind his lips. He'd been away for so long that he really didn't know Margot anymore — or his father, for that matter.

"You know, this store is all I have," his dad said. "After your mum died, after you left. It's all I have, and all I ever had."

Groups of people passed by, most of them completely oblivious to the fact that they were looking at the last two members of the Carroll family.

"I'm not going to live for ever," the old man went on. "And when I do go, this is what I leave the world. My father trusted me to run this place, and I have. It's bigger now than ever. I thought I could trust you to run it too, after I go. You were so happy here when you were a kid. This place was your world. I thought you would trust it to your own children one day too, and they to theirs."

"Dad . . ." Christian said.

"It needs a Carroll!" his dad shouted, coughing hard. "And unluckily for me, I've only got one. But one is all it takes. Is it really too much to ask? Is this life really so awful?"

"I said I'd stay," Christian said, feeling the same spark of anger he always felt when he was talking to his dad. "Until the ship has righted itself. I said I'd stay until then."

"And then what? Back to the Philippines? To mud huts and sewers?"

His dad broke into coughs again, putting a hand on a shelf to steady himself. People were starting to pay attention to him now, and he smiled at a group of older ladies, keeping his voice low.

Then, for a beat, Christian's mind betrayed him. He saw Merry's smile and felt the way his body had lit up when she smiled at him. He could still remember the soft scent of her, the way her breath had hitched when she leaned in. He imagined kissing her, imagined what it would be like to sink into her, to forget everything else for one stolen moment. And that was the problem. Because for a second he let himself wonder if there might actually be something here worth staying for.

The thought hit him like a punch to the chest.

No. Absolutely not.

He had to get out of here. Before he did something stupid and let a pretty girl and a pile of unresolved guilt convince him that he could make peace with this life. Because he couldn't. He knew what this place did to people. What it had done to him.

He turned on his heel before his father could respond, needing space to breathe, needing to remember that just because something felt good didn't mean it was right. Because the truth was, if he didn't leave soon, he might not leave at all.

CHAPTER 11

MERRY

For a day that had started off just about as badly as it could have, things had gone further downhill surprisingly quickly.

For a start, once Merry had escaped the bathroom and returned to Jewellery, the lines for the checkout were so long that people were actually yelling at one another — and at her. Twice she had a complete stranger growl in her face that they were going to take their business elsewhere, and at least three people had put in complaints to the management about the slow service. Merry only discovered this when Mrs Cradley arrived, two hours or so after the incident in the restroom, pulling her away from her station and into the service corridor.

"Look," Merry said, trying to get in front of the old lady. "I'm sorry. I know what you're going to say."

"Hush yourself!" Mrs Cradley barked, flapping her clipboard in Merry's face as if she meant to use it as a weapon. "You seem to think that this job is your leisure time, that you are free to chat idly to friends and acquaintances instead of actually working. But let me tell you something, Miss Sinclair,

71

you are on thin ice. Your job is to satisfy every demand the customer makes of you, and no more. When one task is finished, you move on to the next. And you do not, under any circumstances, physically threaten a visitor to this store."

"I didn't—" she said, but once again Mrs Cradley interrupted her.

"Luckily for you, Mr Carroll himself took care of the incident and found that nobody was at fault, but that was your last warning. Am I making myself clear?"

"As ice," Merry said. "It won't ever happen again."

Mrs Cradley gave her a stern look, then marched away. She had only made it a few yards, however, when she turned back. "And do not use the facilities on this floor," she said. "One of the toilets has exploded."

Then she was gone. Merry took a deep, shuddering breath, then ran back to her position.

A telling-off from Mrs Cradley was nothing new, she thought as she packed up a pair of gold and ruby earrings for a woman in a fur coat. But what was odd was Dragon Lady letting her off so easily after the incident with the horrible couple. Sure, it hadn't been Merry's fault, but they would definitely have mentioned it had been her serving — they would have made her look bad. And they definitely would have accused Christian of assaulting them with a mop. So why had the case been dropped so quickly? And why had the big boss himself, Lewis Carroll, got involved?

It didn't matter. The important thing was that she was off the hook — for that at least. But what about Christian? Mrs Cradley had said that nobody was at fault, but was she just talking about the shop floor staff? Would he lose his job? She wished she could find him and ask him if he was okay, but things were too hectic.

And she didn't just want to find him to check on him. She wanted to find him to see if what had happened — what had *almost* happened — in the bathroom was just a fluke, or if there genuinely was something between them. She still couldn't quite believe it. She couldn't remember a single time in her entire life where she had almost been touched by someone and felt her entire body electrified. It had been like she was on wheels, racing downhill.

You sound like a crazy person, Merry! she silently yelled to herself as she smiled at the next customer. *Enough with the fairy tales!*

She tried to put him out of her mind, but it was a useless battle because every time she blinked she saw him smiling at her, and every time she breathed she thought she smelled his citrus scent. She managed to keep her mind on the job for the rest of her shift, the department so busy that she didn't even have time to take her break. By the time seven o'clock rolled around she was exhausted, starving and her mouth felt like it was lined with sandpaper.

"I'm sorry," she said hoarsely to the next customer. "Somebody will be with you very shortly."

He started to argue, but she broke away and practically ran out of the department, escaping into the staff corridor. Her head was pounding. She pulled off the Santa hat and massaged her temples. As she was waiting for the elevator, she heard a rumble of wheels, and her heart leaped into her throat as she recognised the sound of a janitor's trolley.

It was Christian. He'd been waiting for her.

She ran a hand through her chaotic hair, grinning her sweetest smile as a man in blue overalls emerged from the stock room door.

It wasn't Christian. It was Harvey, an older, portly janitor who Merry always said hi to in passing. He caught sight of her beaming smile and one appeared on his own wrinkled face.

"Now if that ain't the sweetest thing I've ever seen," he said, limping towards her. "Honestly, if people greeted one another every day with a smile like that there wouldn't be no trouble in the world."

If anything, his words made Merry's smile even wider. It hadn't been meant for the old janitor, but no smile was ever a waste of time, and if it had brightened his day then it had brightened hers too.

The elevator doors opened, and she held them for him. "Going up?" she asked.

"Yes, miss," he replied. "Thank you."

She entered after him and the service elevator grumbled upwards.

"You done for the day?" Harvey asked.

"Yes, thankfully," she said. "That was a tough shift."

"Uh-huh, it always is this close to Christmas, and there doesn't seem to be anyone working anymore."

"Yeah, right?" Merry said. "I thought that too. Where is everyone?"

Harvey shrugged, wiping his red, tired eyes. "People come and people go. That's the way life works."

"Speaking of which," she said as the elevator continued to rise, "do you know anything about the new guy? The one on your team?"

"Chris?" Harvey said, and she nodded. "Oh, sure, seems like a nice young man. Very polite, very thorough. Thought it was weird how he was taken on so soon after another three janitors were let go, but the management must have their reasons. He's certainly a credit to the store, and a good man."

His words reassured Merry. Christian *was* a good man, she was utterly convinced of it. Some people just revealed the quality of their nature in everything they did, in every word, in every smile, in every movement.

"It's just a shame he ain't hanging around," said Harvey.

The elevator suddenly felt twenty degrees cooler.

"What?" Merry asked.

Harvey pulled out a cloth from his pocket and wiped his nose, sniffing. "Chris," he said. "He ain't staying. This is a temporary job, it always was. He came on board to cover the janitors who left, he says, but it's only until Christmas. After that everything will quiet down."

"How do you know that?" Christian hadn't mentioned leaving at all, but then they hadn't really talked about the future, and there was no reason he'd have wanted to discuss it.

"He told me." Harvey glanced suspiciously at Merry, as if she was a police sergeant and he was a perp. "He told all of us he was only here till the end of the year. Why so curious?"

"Oh, no reason."

The elevator slowed to a halt, the doors sliding open on the tenth floor. Harvey wheeled his trolley out, stopping when she called out to him.

"Where is he going after that?"

"Back home," said the man. "Back to the Philippines."

He trundled away, leaving Merry feeling as if she had plummeted back down through the cold, dark elevator shaft. She wrapped her arms around herself protectively, feeling echoes of the same dreadful hurt she'd felt so many times in her short life. But that was unfair to Christian — he didn't owe her anything.

The elevator doors started to close, and she rushed through them. The staff area was relatively busy as people finished their day shifts and the evening clerks came in, and Merry weaved her way down the corridor into the locker rooms. She was too tired to change, so she grabbed her clothes and her coat. She was hoping that she'd bump into Christian on the way out. Part of her wanted to ask him out for hot chocolate again — especially so she could find out whether Harvey was right about him leaving soon — but part of her knew it would be better for everyone if she stayed out of his way. If she didn't see him again, then it wouldn't be so heartbreaking when he left the country.

Heartbreaking? Merry tutted at herself. How could she have her heart broken by a man she'd known for less than two days? It was ridiculous. It had to be the fact that it was Christmas, she thought. Even though Adrian had done his best to ruin it for her for ever, Merry still wanted to believe. All those Christmas romcoms where the couples fall in love, all those Hallmark cards, all those commercials showing people snuggling up in front of log fires, eating sugar cookies and opening presents together.

But none of that was real. Christmas was a lie used to sell people stuff they didn't want or need. She could see that every single day, working here. She could see what it really meant.

Merry pushed through the door on to the shop floor, angry at herself for her cynicism, and sad too that she had lost a part of herself. Once upon a time she had loved Christmas so much, had revelled in the glorious sentimentality of it. Once upon a time she had thought that anything was possible at Christmas, that it was a time for love and joy and happiness and hope. Now, though . . .

Now it was just a time for disappointment.

As if to prove her point, Santa's grotto was closed, the lights dimmed and a chain drawn over the entrance. Harvey was busy mopping the floor and he nodded to her as she walked past. Merry did her best to smile back, but then a familiar, snappy voice plunged her even deeper into despair.

"Miss Sinclair?"

Oh, no. Just keep walking, pretend you can't hear her! she ordered herself.

Then Mrs Cradley called her name again and she turned to face her.

"Are you sure your shift has ended?" the Dragon Lady asked, checking her watch.

"Yes," Merry said. "Like, forty minutes ago. I couldn't get off the floor."

"Well, if you would be so kind, I need you to do one last thing for me."

Merry blew out a breath. All she really wanted to do was go home and draw a bath. But then she thought of her cold apartment, the empty rooms, the stack of unpaid bills.

"Fine. What do you need?"

"There are some items for lost property in the grotto," said Mrs Cradley, smiling as if she was enjoying her role as chief tormentor. "Please collect them and take them to the information desk in the lobby."

"Sure," said Merry, wondering why the Dragon Lady hadn't asked any one of the other three members of staff she could still see on duty.

Mrs Cradley nodded curtly, then spun on her heels and marched away.

Merry shuffled wearily back across the children's department, ducking under the chain and opening the door of the little hut where Santa's gifts were stocked. She had walked inside, muttering under her breath, before she noticed that she wasn't alone.

"Oh, I'm sorry," she said to the man dressed as Santa. He was sitting on a little stool in the corner of the hut, sipping tea from a mug. "I thought you'd already left."

Santa lifted a hand to wave away her apology. He smiled at her, his eyes twinkling in the half-light. She'd caught glimpses of the man over the last few weeks, sitting on his chair and handing gifts to the children, but only now did she notice what a good Santa Claus he was. The Santas she remembered from her own childhood shopping trips were all skinny and tall, with obvious padding in their fading costumes and wisps of brown hair visible beneath their wiry white wigs. But this guy was almost the real deal. His beard was thick and full, a snow-coloured cloud of curls. His cheeks were rosy and his eyes were bright blue and perfectly clear behind the little round spectacles. He laughed kindly, and the 'ho ho ho!' of it was right out of a movie.

"Don't worry about me," he said in a deep, friendly voice. "I'm just enjoying a cup of tea before I head back to the North Pole."

Merry's laugh was surprisingly genuine. "That sounds like a long journey after a long day."

"Oh, it's not too long at all," he replied, "when you have reindeer to carry you and a little magic to help you on your way."

He winked, and she laughed again.

"I'm here for the lost property," she said, and Santa pretended to be sad.

"Is that all? It seems to me that you might be looking for something else — a bit of Christmas spirit, perhaps?"

Merry shook her head. "This is Fifth Avenue, not 34th Street. My days of believing in you have long gone."

Santa put a hand to his chest. "It always breaks my heart to hear people say that. For although you might have stopped believing in me, I never stop believing in you. Come here."

He placed his mug on the floor, beckoning her over.

"I really can't," she said, feeling the ache in her legs and back. "I've got to get this stuff down to Lost Property, then head home. I've been here for ever."

"Grant me this one little wish," Santa said, insistent.

Merry hung her head, then walked across the small room, the floorboards creaking beneath her feet.

Santa smiled up at her. "Don't worry, you don't have to sit on my lap. Just give me your hand, if that's okay with you?"

"Look . . ." Merry started, but Santa reached out and took her hand in his own. His palms were soft and leathery, and he held her hand gently in both of his.

"Merry," he said, smiling at her. "Of all the people here, surely you must still have faith in Christmas?"

"How did you know my name?" she asked.

Santa's eyes twinkled. "You're still wearing your name tag."

Merry laughed again. Santa held her hands gently. "I want you to close your eyes and try to remember what it was like to be a child. Remember that feeling of excitement, and of deep, loving comfort you always had on Christmas Eve, then the joy of Christmas morning."

"Come on," Merry said. She couldn't quite believe this was happening, but the man was so kind, his voice so soothing, that she decided to play along. "Okay, sure."

She closed her eyes and thought back to being a kid, lying in bed in Nebraska, the thick snow outside plunging the world into silence, the glow of the Christmas lights outside turning her room red, then green, then gold. Every year she'd vowed to stay up and meet Santa when he arrived to deliver her presents, and every year she'd fallen asleep sitting up in bed. And that feeling of waking up on Christmas Day — did anything ever really beat that? That moment where the fog of sleep faded away and you suddenly remembered what day it was. Despite herself, Merry giggled.

"That's it!" said Santa. "I knew you still had a little magic inside you. Now quickly, while it's there, tell me what you would like for Christmas."

"What?" Merry asked, smiling at the man.

Santa smiled back. "Your present, what would you like?"

"Uh . . ." Merry shrugged. "I haven't really thought about it. I don't know."

"Yes, you do," he said quietly.

There were lots of things she needed. Her coffee machine had broken, the shower was leaking and her shoes were practically worn out from all the walking she did in this place.

"Think about what you *really* want," the man asked.

As soon as he'd said it, Christian's face appeared in Merry's mind. And even though she barely knew him, even though he was probably going to be leaving the country in a few weeks, even though there couldn't possibly be a future for them, she made a wish — a wish that she could spend Christmas with him.

"I just want to be happy," she said, opening her eyes.

"And you will be." Santa gave her hands one last squeeze before letting go. "You will be, Merry."

Gradually, the real world faded back in — the sound of Harvey's mop cleaning the floor, somebody making an announcement over the public address system. Merry laughed, but this time it felt a little self-conscious. She was aware of the cardboard walls and roof of the hut, the fake snow that lay on the ground, and she knew that Santa was just as much of an imitation.

But still, something in her had changed. Whatever the man had done, he'd ignited the smallest flame, a tiny flicker of hope that glowed like an open fire on a dark night. Maybe, just maybe, her wish might come true.

"Believe," Santa said, as if he was reading her mind. "Go on now, and have a very Merry Christmas."

"You too," Merry said, collecting the bag of lost property and opening the door.

Santa laughed, his kind voice following her out. "I always do."

CHAPTER 12

CHRISTIAN

Christian checked his watch as he paced. It was coming up for half past seven and he still hadn't seen her. Fifth Avenue was dark and drenched and absolutely heaving with people. It was raining so hard it was impossible to see to the other side of the street, and Carroll's Department Store had three main entrances, not to mention the staff access doors and loading areas around the back. He didn't even know what time Merry got off work — for all he knew she'd slipped out already.

What are you doing? he asked himself, wiping the rain from his face. At least he'd had the good sense to pick up another jacket, given Merry still had his lumberjack and the temperature had dropped another few degrees overnight. It was an old Hermès, but he hoped it wouldn't be too obvious.

He'd gotten off work an hour ago, and he hadn't managed to stop thinking about the conversation with his father. He didn't know how to explain it, just that the idea of staying felt too complicated and heavy.

All he knew was that the one thing tempting him to even think about staying was Merry. That and the fact that every time he thought about her, something cinched tight in his chest. Someone had ruined Christmas for her, and though he knew it was dangerous, Christian wanted to make it better before he left.

A gust of bitterly cold wind tore up the street and he pulled his jacket tight around his neck, shivering. A group of people came out of Carroll's, holding bags and moaning about the weather. He squinted into the store, trying hopelessly to find Merry in the crowds.

"You look like you've been swimming in the Hudson."

The voice startled him, and he spun around like he was being attacked.

"Whoa!" Merry flinched at his sudden movement. "I'm not going to headbutt you again, I promise."

"Merry!" To his immense astonishment, she was there, wearing his lumberjack coat, the hood pulled up, and her eyes gleaming from the shadows.

"The one and only," she replied. "What are you doing out here?"

"Waiting," he said, too flabbergasted to form a complete sentence.

"Waiting for what? If you don't mind me asking?"

"Uh . . ." He paused, cocking his head. "You."

Merry started to laugh. "Wait, what?" Her teeth tugged at her bottom lip. "Me? You're standing on Fifth Avenue in the cold and the rain waiting for me?"

Christian nodded, his pulse racing like the engines of the taxis that roared past.

"Why?" she asked, as if it was the most unbelievable thing in the world that anyone would want to see her.

"I have a plan," he said. "If you are willing."

She lifted an eyebrow. "A plan?"

He shoved his hands deep into his wet pockets. "I wanted to kidnap you for the night."

Her eyes widened and he rushed on. "Not in a weird way. In a Christmas way."

Merry blinked. "A Christmas way?"

He grinned. "You said you weren't feeling it this year. Christmas. New York. All of it. I thought that maybe I could change your mind."

Merry was silent, staring at him through the rain. For a moment, he thought he'd gone too far. Then she pushed her hood back, letting the droplets bead across her hair. "What did you have in mind?"

He smiled wider, feeling the shift, the small miracle of it. "Come with me and find out."

He hailed a cab and they climbed in out of the drizzle, sitting in the warmth as the driver honked his way across town, shouting so loudly it was impossible to have a conversation. The cab pulled to a juddering halt, Christian paid and ran around to open the door for Merry with a little bow, like they were stepping into a ballroom instead of a crowded Midtown sidewalk.

"Oh, wow," Merry breathed, taking Christian's hand as she climbed out of the cab and into the glittering wonderland of Bryant Park Winter Village.

It was utterly magnificent. Strings of red and green bulbs glittered like jewels through the mist, and the scent of roasted chestnuts drifted over from a nearby vendor. Christian didn't say anything. He just watched her face light up.

"Okay," she said, turning to him with wide eyes. "This was a good idea."

The air was thick with the delicious aromas of sizzling meats, cinnamon sugar, melted cheese and spiced cider. Strings of lights criss-crossed overhead, glittering like stars. The booths were bustling, music spilling from speakers, and people wrapped in scarves smiled as they queued. Merry stopped short, soaking it all in.

"Wow," she said again.

"See?" Christian nodded, watching her face more than the lights. "This evening is going to be edible Christmas therapy."

He gestured ahead, and together they strolled down the main path, winding between stalls and waving fairy lights. Just

83

ahead, the ice rink stretched out in the centre of the village, ringed by benches and glowing trees.

"Corn dogs, cheesesteaks or raclette?" he asked casually as they passed a booth selling miniature ornaments shaped like pickles and tiny sushi rolls.

She raised an eyebrow. "You're giving me a choice?"

"This is serious business," he said. "Festive reawakening must be done properly."

Merry smiled, her cheeks pink from the cold.

They paused at the edge of the rink, watching the skaters loop and spin and cling to the sides. One kid fell spectacularly, then immediately broke into laughter. His dad helped him up, steadying him by the elbows before they set off again together.

"I used to love skating " Merry said softly, leaning against the railing. "Haven't done it in years. Last time I went I got taken out by a guy doing a triple spin and landed flat on my back. Very festive."

Christian winced in sympathy. "I once tried to impress a girl in high school by skating backwards in front of her. Wiped out, took her down with me, and broke her phone with my knee."

Merry snorted. "You're really bad at impressing women, huh?"

"I've gotten better," he said, nudging her shoulder with his own. "I hope."

"I'll let you know at the end of the night." Merry didn't seem to see the effect her words had on Christian, or if she did she was playing it cool. "You know this market is like a celebrity in its own right? Every year I say I'm going to come see it, and every year I get too busy or too cold or too—"

"Grinchy?"

She gave him a playful glare. "Did you just say grinchy?"

"Might have." He smirked. "But I was right, yeah?"

She shook her head, but she was smiling. "Maybe a little."

He tilted his head towards her. "On a scale of one to Whoville, how grinchy are we talking?"

"Mid-grinch," she admitted.

"Let's aim for full Cindy Lou Who by midnight."

A violinist on the corner began playing a slow, lilting version of 'Have Yourself a Merry Little Christmas' and, for a moment, everything around them hushed. They stood there, quietly, wrapped in the twinkle and hum of the city. Skaters spun below them, laughter echoing up from the rink, and the lights overhead seemed to pulse in time with the music.

Merry gave a little sigh, one that misted softly in the air.

"I know it's cheesy," she said, "but it's kind of perfect, isn't it?"

They lingered a moment longer, soaking in the music, the laughter, the slice of skates against ice. Then the wind brought a new wave of mouthwatering scent from down the path.

"Okay, my stomach is screaming at me, and that cheese-steak place smells insane," Merry said, eyes bright.

Christian's grin widened. "Excellent choice."

The line for the truffle cheesesteaks wasn't short, but neither of them minded. The smells were intoxicating and, as they waited, Merry leaned casually against Christian's side, making him hyper-aware of every point of contact.

"This might be the best decision I've made all week," she murmured, watching a staffer behind the counter shovel grilled onions on to a bun.

Christian glanced at her, the string lights casting a golden glow across her cheeks. "I'd like it noted for the record that I brought you here."

"Oh, you want credit already?"

"I want a plaque," he said. "'Christian: Restorer of Christmas Spirit. Bringer of Cheesesteaks.'"

She laughed, head tipped back slightly, and he felt the heat rise in his chest. Their sandwiches arrived wrapped in brown paper, still steaming from the grill. Merry peeled hers open and her eyes grew wide. "Oh my God."

Christian bit into his. The flavours hit so hard he let out a satisfied sigh.

Merry took her first bite and let out a noise that was halfway indecent. Christian's brain stalled. He tried to recover, but his mouth was full and his body had already decided that whatever that sound was, it was very much his business. Merry caught the look on his face and laughed, covering her mouth with the back of her hand.

"Oh my God," she said, a little breathless. "Sorry, that was uncalled for. It's just, this is literally orgasmic."

"Right?" he said, swallowing hard. "And your little moan was—"

"Embarrassing?" she interrupted, nose wrinkled.

"Not the word I'd use." He took another bite just to give himself something to do, but it was too late. Every nerve in his body was paying attention now.

They stood under the awning of the stall, pressed shoulder to shoulder as they ate, sauce dripping on to their napkins, and when Merry went to take another bite, the cheese stretched out across her hands and down her chin.

Christian handed her an extra napkin. "You've got cheese on your—"

She took it and wiped blindly at her cheek. "Did I get it?"

"Close," he said, then reached over and ran a thumb over her chin. She froze, watching him for a second too long. Her lips parted, just a little, but enough to make Christian's chest hitch at the sight of her perfect pout. Oh, the things he'd like to do to that mouth.

She cleared her throat. "Okay. So, we need drinks to wash this down. Cider?"

"Cider," he confirmed, heart thudding. "This way."

They made their way towards the drinks stand as they finished their sandwiches. The air was still damp but no longer biting, filled now with laughter, 'Jingle Bells' and the faint hum of festive music crackling from overhead speakers.

Christian ordered two hot apple ciders, both crowned with a towering swirl of whipped cream and cinnamon, and a side of half a donut glistening with sugar.

"Careful," he said, handing a cup to Merry. "They said it's lava."

Merry gripped hers between her gloved hands, inhaling deeply. "Thanks," she said, looking intensely at her drink. She hadn't met his eye since he had touched her and a part of him wondered if he'd overstepped the mark.

The worry settled low in his gut. He wasn't exactly a master of restraint, especially around her. But he didn't want to make her uncomfortable. He was thinking about how to apologise when Merry turned to him, frowning. "I know you're leaving," she blurted out.

Christian blinked. "What?"

Merry finally looked up at him. "You're not staying in New York, are you?"

His breath caught, and for a second, he considered lying. But something in her face told him not to. So, he simply nodded. "After Christmas."

Her gaze dropped to her cider. She gave it a little swirl, whipped cream sliding down into the cup.

"I heard. I just wasn't sure if you were going to tell me. Not that it's any of my business."

"It is," he said quietly. "I wasn't sure how to bring it up. And I wasn't sure if you'd come here with me this evening if you knew."

Her mouth twitched, like she was fighting a smile. "I knew and I'm still here."

"Right." He shifted closer, the noise of the market somehow fading beneath the weight of this moment. "I wanted to give you something before I go. Something Christmassy. Because when you told me you'd fallen out of love with the holidays, I couldn't let that go. I didn't want to leave without trying to fix that."

"You're not responsible for fixing my Christmas spirit," she said. "That's not your job."

"I know," he said. "But I wanted to anyway."

She didn't reply right away, just looked at him, and in the silence, Christian felt dangerously close to wanting more than he knew he should. She blew gently across the surface of her drink, then took a slow, careful sip. The moment the heat hit her tongue, she gave a quiet, contented sigh that went straight to Christian's bloodstream.

And then, God help him, the whipped cream caught on her lip. Just a little. A pale puff clinging to the corner of her mouth, like frosting on a cake. Christian stopped breathing. Merry didn't notice at first. She licked the edge of the cup, then used the tip of her tongue to sweep the cream from her lip with devastating effect on Christian's self-control.

He looked away, then immediately looked back, gripping his own cup harder than was strictly necessary.

"This is so good," she murmured. "Sweet, and tart, and a little spicy. Honestly, if someone put this in a perfume bottle, I'd wear it."

Christian tried to answer, but the words tangled somewhere between *"You already smell incredible"* and *"I am in so much trouble."*

Merry took another sip, then smiled around the rim. "Why does everything taste better tonight?"

"Maybe because you're actually letting yourself enjoy it," he said, more serious than he had intended.

She glanced up, surprised. Their eyes met and, just like that, the noise of the market faded, the lights blurred and the space between them hummed with something warm and magnetic. Everything slowed down. Not a single person bumped them, even though the path buzzed with life. It felt like they were standing in the centre of something only they could feel.

"I like being with you," Merry said quietly, her voice barely rising above the murmur of the crowd. "Maybe more than I should — and that feels dangerous."

Christian swallowed hard. "Dangerous how?"

"Like I might forget you're leaving." The ache in her voice rooted him to the spot. "And I don't want to forget."

Christian's chest tightened. "I haven't left yet, Merry."

The air between them thrummed and, in that moment, all he could think about was how easy it would be to kiss her.

To take her hand, hail a cab and pull her back to his hotel room. Her flushed cheeks, the shine of cider still on her lips, it was all driving him to the edge.

Too much, he thought. *Too soon.*

"Come on." He nudged her gently. "There's something else I want to show you."

Merry blinked, like she'd forgotten where they were. "What is it?"

He offered his arm, managing a crooked smile. "Bryant Park's Christmas tree. Some people say it's better than Rockefeller's."

She looked almost relieved by the shift. "Better how?"

"Less flashy, more heart." He gave her a sideways glance. "Kind of like you."

Merry shook her head, smiling as she looped her arm through his. "You're such a flirt."

He leaned in as they began walking. "You have no idea."

He could have sworn he heard her huff out a little breath, but he forced himself to ignore it as they wandered along the paths, past booths of handmade ornaments and tiny carved animals until they reached the tree.

It stood tall at the centre end of the park, a glowing tower of warm white lights, snowflakes, stars and deep red ribbons that curled and looped like sugar candy.

"Oh," Merry said softly. "Wow."

Christian glanced at her, but she was mesmerised by the tree, watching the lights twinkle like stars strung from the branches.

"I used to think Christmas trees were magic," Merry murmured. "Like, they weren't just decorations but that they meant something homely and safe."

"And now?"

"Now I think I just forgot how to look at them," she whispered.

He gently bumped her with his shoulder. "I think you're remembering."

She looked up at him, her expression unreadable. "Maybe I am."

For a moment neither of them moved. Christian had the overwhelming urge to lean down and kiss Merry, to pull her closer and freezeframe the time before it slipped away.

"Dessert?" Christian asked, instead, after a beat.

"I can't eat anything else," Merry declared, one hand pressed dramatically to her stomach. "If I so much as smell another pastry, I might combust."

Christian laughed. "Agreed. But we still need dessert."

She turned to him, eyes wide. "We had some."

"Nope," he said. "That was pre-dessert cider and donuts. This is dessert dessert."

She narrowed her eyes. "You're making this up."

"Not at all. It's a thing. And look—" He pointed behind them to a stall glowing with giant red-and-white candy canes, shiny and thick, stacked like festive swords. "Perfect."

Merry let out a soft laugh. "You're not serious."

"Deadly," he said. "A proper finale. Plus, we don't have to eat them all at once."

She rolled her eyes but followed him to the counter, letting him pay for a pair of oversized canes. Christian watched her as she slowly unwrapped hers, peeling the plastic back inch by inch and then sliding the end between her lips. Big mistake.

"Spicy," she said. "Cinnamon. That's a surprise."

He opened his mouth to respond but nothing came out. She licked along the side of it thoughtfully. "I like it."

Christian's brain short-circuited. Every drop of blood in his body seemed to redirect southward. He was barely still standing.

He needed to capture this moment for ever. He whipped out his phone and told Merry to smile.

Merry smiled for the camera, tongue still on the candy cane, innocently oblivious to what she was doing to him. "You okay?"

"Fine," he said, voice higher than normal. "Totally fine."

He tried to focus on the lights, on the chill in the air, anything that wasn't the obscene beauty of her mouth wrapped around a piece of candy.

She looked at him sideways, her smile just a little wicked. "Are you blushing?"

He gave her a crooked grin, trying to play it cool even as he fought the urge to shift in place. "Not even slightly."

"Hmm." She popped the candy cane back into her mouth. "That's a shame. I'll have to try harder."

CHAPTER 13

MERRY

Maybe it was the cider or the sheer absurd joy of the night, but something inside her had snapped loose. She wanted to kiss him. Hard. Wanted to throw caution so far to the wind it might never find its way back. She parted her lips slightly and tilted her face towards his, heart hammering.

Then the sky cracked open.

It didn't just rain, it slammed down like a curtain dropping mid-scene, drenching them in seconds. The Christmas lights blurred, candy-cane red and white twisting in watery streaks.

"Jesus Christ!" she yelped, bursting into laughter as the cold hit her like a freight train.

Christian let out a strangled shout, one hand flying up over his head in a pathetic attempt to shield himself. "I knew I should've brought an umbrella!"

"You're a native New Yorker," she laughed, grabbing his arm and tugging. "Aren't you supposed to own this?"

The market was already dissolving into chaos with vendors yanking down tarps and people screaming and scattering like chickens. He gripped her hand in his and they ran. Merry's feet slapped against the pavement, her hand locked in Christian's, their laughter echoing through the sudden storm. Rain poured from the sky, soaking her to the bone, but she didn't care.

It was electric. *He* was electric.

"There!" Christian pointed towards the subway entrance just across the street.

They dashed for it, slipping past slower-moving crowds and dodging umbrellas that had become useless in the downpour. Merry's hair clung to her cheeks, her breath fogging in the air as they flew down the steps, water sluicing off their clothes.

At the bottom, she stumbled to a halt beside Christian, breathless and dripping. They stared at each other, soaked to the skin, cheeks flushed from the cold and the sprint and their proximity.

"Are you okay?" he asked, breath catching.

She nodded. "Are you?"

He shrugged, chest rising and falling. "Never better."

The subway was packed with damp people clutching umbrellas and dripping bags, shoulders hunched against the wet. The fluorescent lights buzzed overhead, casting everything in a sickly, flickering glow.

Merry stood on the edge of the platform, every nerve ending lit up as the train screamed into the station, brakes shrieking, and when the doors opened it was like a stampede. They got swept inside, barely managing to stay upright, squashed between a businessman with a soaked briefcase and a teenager blasting music through one earbud.

Christian ended up behind her, his body pressed fully against her back. The jolt of the train starting up rocked them even closer, and she felt every hard plane of him, the heat of his breath against the back of her neck.

Merry gripped the cold metal pole beside her so hard her knuckles ached. Her other hand hung useless at her side, twitching with the need to reach for him. Her clothes were soaked through, her skin cold, but every inch that touched him was burning.

Christian shifted, almost imperceptibly, and she felt the slow drag of his breath as his mouth brushed her temple soft enough to make a heat curl low and hot between her thighs. The train jolted and someone cursed as another passenger bumped against her. Christian's arm moved fast, anchoring her to him. His hand splayed low over her stomach, holding her steadily against his chest.

Merry closed her eyes.

What are we doing? Where is this going? Do I even care anymore?

The train screeched into her station and she grabbed Christian's hand without a word. His skin was hot as she pulled him through the crowd, weaving past slow-moving commuters with single-minded urgency. Neither of them spoke as they exited into the night. The rain was still coming down hard, slanting sideways beneath the streetlights. By the time they reached her building, the silence between them was vibrating with something exhilarating.

She stopped at the front door, keys already in hand, her pulse roaring in her ears. For a moment she didn't move. Just stood there with her back to him, breath catching, one hand trembling on the lock. Then his hand slid over hers. The other ghosted along her waist, drawing her gently back against him as the key scraped softly in the lock.

He lowered his head to her ear. "Are you sure you want to do this?" he whispered.

Merry answered him by turning the key and Christian made a sound low in his throat. A half-groan, half-growl that went straight through her.

Her breath came fast as she toed off her boots, fingers trembling slightly as she pulled off her coat. His coat. She turned, walking silently through the short hallway towards her bedroom. She could feel him behind her and was suddenly aware of every imperfect detail — the laundry basket half-full

94

in the corner, the faint smell of lavender fabric softener, and the icy frost that had crept across the inside of her bedroom window.

She hesitated at the door, just for a second, feeling a wave of embarrassment rise up at the sight of it. A thin sheen of vulnerability exposed. Before she could say anything, Christian stepped in close behind her. His voice was low and rough against her damp shoulder.

"You look like a gift," he murmured, his mouth brushing her skin, her door clicking gently shut behind them. "And I'm going to take my time unwrapping you."

Before she could catch her breath, he spun her around and pressed his mouth on hers. Soaked from the rain, their bodies collided like they'd been waiting a lifetime. His hands found her hair, pulling her closer like he couldn't get enough. The kiss deepened instantly, his tongue finding hers. Merry gasped in pleasure against his mouth, and he swallowed the sound with a groan that vibrated all the way through her.

Her uniform was soaked, clinging to every curve, and when they finally pulled apart, his eyes dropped to the outline of her breasts. Under the weight of his stare, her nipples pebbled visibly beneath the thin cotton.

"Merry," he whispered. "Look at you."

She reached for the zip at the side of her dress, but his hands were already there.

"Let me," he said, voice low. "I've been thinking about this since the second I saw you in that uniform."

Merry's stomach flipped. She lifted her arms, letting him peel the sodden dress over her head inch by inch. The wet fabric clung like glue, and the friction only made it hotter. Dropping the dress to the floor he lowered his mouth to the hollow of her throat and began kissing every drop of water that trailed down her body. One at her collarbone. Another between the swell of her breasts still wrapped in her bra.

His fingers slid behind her back and the clasp of her bra gave instantly. It slipped down her arms and hit the floor without a sound. His eyes dropped, and her nipples tightened into harder peaks under the heat of his gaze.

He reached up and cupped her breasts in both hands, his thumbs stroking slowly over each nipple. The touch was electric and she felt it through her core. She gasped, arching into his hands, chasing the contact, but he stopped and took a step back, drinking her in with his eyes.

"Christian," she whispered, the word barely a breath, but it seemed to snap the last thread of his control.

He reached for the hem of his own jumper and yanked it over his head in one fluid motion, water splashing across the floor. Merry's mouth went dry. His chest was broad and cut, skin slick from the rain, abs tight and defined, the kind of body sculpted by effort and, right now, it was all hers.

Christian saw the way her eyes devoured him, the way her thighs pressed together, and a slow, wicked grin curled at the corner of his mouth.

He undid the button on his jeans with one slow flick. The rasp of the zipper followed, impossibly loud in the quiet room. He pushed them down his hips, the soaked denim dragging over hard muscle, revealing the thick outline of him beneath black boxers.

Within seconds he was completely naked and unapologetically hard. His cock stood thick and flushed, curved up towards his stomach, already leaking at the tip. He was big. And there wasn't a single part of him that didn't look ready to ruin her in the best possible way.

She swallowed hard, heat surging through her, her thighs instinctively pressing tighter as she throbbed with want. Christian caught the movement and his grin turned feral.

Still watching her, he wrapped a hand around his cock, fingers tightening at the base as he gave himself one slow, possessive tug. Every nerve in her body locked on to that one motion and she reached for him without thinking, desperate to touch him.

But he stepped just out of reach.

"Not yet."

Her hand froze mid-air, trembling.

"I told you, I'm unwrapping this slowly."

He sank to his knees in front of her, hands sliding up the outsides of her thighs, thumbs hooking just under the waistband of her tights. The fabric clung to her, damp and tight, but he took his time. Inch by inch, he eased them down her legs, dragging them over her hips, her thighs, grazing every new inch of bare skin with his thumbs as he went.

She gripped the edge of the dresser behind her, legs wobbling. When he got to her knees, he leaned in, hot breath ghosting over the inside of her thighs. Merry whimpered, her hips twitching forward, but Christian didn't rush.

He kissed the inside of one thigh, then the other, then lower, pressing open-mouthed kisses down the line of her leg as he peeled the tights further, past her knees, down her calves. By the time he reached her ankles and slipped the damp fabric off completely, she was shaking.

Then he rose and caught her mouth in a kiss that was nothing like the last. This one was hungry. His tongue swept into her mouth like he meant to devour her. His hands locked around her hips, holding her still as she melted against him, her bare chest pressing to his, nipples grazing his skin with every breath.

The friction was maddening. She arched into him, chasing more, her body aching for his hands, his mouth, anything he'd give her.

He trailed his fingers between their bodies and found the lace edges of her panties. He tugged at them gently, stroking across the fabric with maddening lightness. His fingers found her centre through the soaked cotton, pressing gently, and she heard him breathe out a low chuckle.

He took a step back, eyes locked on hers. "You good?" he asked, breathily. "Tell me now, Merry. You want me to stop?"

"Don't you dare."

Something dark and hungry flickered behind his eyes. "Good," he growled. "Because I'm done unwrapping, now it's time to play."

He leaned in and kissed her throat, trailing his mouth down until his lips brushed the top of her breast. Merry shuddered as his mouth closed over one nipple, sucking it deep, tongue circling slowly before giving it a light, deliberate bite. She cried out, the sharpness lighting her nerves on fire.

Before she could recover, he moved to the other — his free hand still cupping her pussy through the wet cotton, keeping her right on the edge while his mouth wrecked her above. He sucked and grazed her with his teeth again, enough to make her hips buck forward into his hand.

"Patience, Merry," he groaned, giving her a light slap on the ass.

The sharp contact made her gasp and sent a fresh, helpless pulse of desire through her. She felt it, hot and slick, between her thighs.

"Fuck your patience," she whispered into his mouth. "Who turned you into a goddam sadist?"

Before she could draw another breath, he dropped his gaze and, with one sharp tug, ripped her panties clean off. The soaked fabric tore in his fist, and he flung them aside. She barely had time to react before his hand was back between her legs, sliding through her folds with a wet sound that made them both groan.

"Fuck, Merry," he gasped, voice hoarse. "You're soaked."

And then he plunged two fingers inside her, deep and hard, just as his thumb found her clit. Her head fell back, a cry bursting from her lips as her body clamped around him, already fluttering with the pleasure she'd been holding in. Her knees buckled, but he caught her, one arm bracing around her back, holding her up like she weighed nothing.

"Stay with me," he murmured, kissing her jaw and her throat, even as his fingers rocked into her.

She gasped his name, his fingers buried deep, each thrust angled just right, sending sparks up her spine. He curled them, hitting that spot over and over while his thumb kept up its relentless rhythm on her clit. It was more pleasure than Merry had ever felt before.

"God, Merry," he growled against her throat. "You feel incredible."

She could only moan, her voice broken, eyes squeezed shut as the pressure spiralled impossibly tight. Every nerve was lit up. Her thighs were shaking. Her body clenched hard around his fingers, so close to pure ecstasy.

"Let go," he whispered, thrusting deeper. "I want to feel you come."

And she did. The orgasm hit like a wave, crashing through her so violently her legs gave out completely. He held her firm, fingers still working her through every last pulse. She cried his name, as pleasure roared through her in a flood.

"You're incredible," Christian rasped, his voice thick and rough against her ear.

CHAPTER 14

CHRISTIAN

His fingers were soaked, still buried deep inside her, as her body fluttered around them in the aftershocks of what he was sure was the hottest fucking orgasm he'd ever witnessed. Merry's breath was coming in ragged little gasps against his shoulder. Her skin was flushed and gleaming, and all of the above was making his cock throb painfully hard.

Jesus Christ.

He slid his fingers free with slow, deliberate care, watching the way her slickness clung to them and how her body flinched at the loss. She didn't even know how gorgeous she was like this.

And right now she's all mine. The thought slammed into him, white-hot.

His gaze snagged on the edge of the dresser behind her. It was the perfect height.

"Hands on the dresser," he murmured against her ear. "Now."

She turned her head eyes still dazed. But she obeyed, moving slowly, her legs still trembling. He caught her hips and helped her pivot, his hands firm as he guided her to bend over the edge. With her palms flattened against the wood, her hair tumbled forward, still damp and clinging to her spine.

And, fuck, the sight of her arched and bare and glistening for him nearly undid him on the spot.

Christian ran a hand down the curve of her back, pausing at the dip of her waist, then lower, to cup her ass. He squeezed once, then spread her gently, revealing her soaked, swollen pussy, still flushed from her climax. His cock jerked in response.

He hissed a breath through his teeth. "You've got no idea what you do to me."

His gaze raked over her one more time, then he straightened and reached for his jacket, still crumpled on the floor beside them. He crouched, found the inner pocket and pulled out the foil square. He tore it open with a flick of his fingers and rolled the condom on with practised ease, his cock hard in his hands. When he looked up, Merry was watching him over her shoulder, her eyes dark, her body still bent over the dresser like a gift he was about to unwrap all over again.

Christian's mouth curved. "Did I tell you I was a boy scout? Always prepared."

Merry huffed a breathless laugh, but it turned into a moan as he stepped back to her, one hand on her hip, the other guiding himself to her soaked, swollen entrance. He ran his cock up her, lubricating the tip on her slick pussy, and pressed inside with one slow, deliberate thrust, filling her inch by inch until his hips met the curve of her ass.

"Oh, Merry," he sighed. "You feel like a fucking dream."

She moaned, pushing back against him instinctively. Christian gritted his teeth, drawing back and thrusting in again, deep and slow, sinking into her like he had all the time in the world.

Each stroke made her gasp, her body still quivering from her orgasm. She was hot and tight around him, and he had to concentrate hard to stop his own release. He wanted more from her first.

He reached around, hand slipping easily between her thighs, fingers finding her pulsing clit. He rubbed slow circles, syncing his touch to the rhythm of his hips, coaxing her higher again.

Merry flinched and let out a sharp breath. "I . . . Christian, I don't think I can come again. I already—"

"Yes, you can." He stopped her, pressing a kiss to her shoulder. "Trust me."

He moved his fingers tenderly with little pressure. Just gentle, knowing strokes as he thrust in and out of her. Merry's body writhed against him, her moans caught between over-stimulation and a new wave building.

"It's perfect," he rasped. "You're perfect. Let it happen."

He buried his face in her neck, breathing her in as he picked up the pace. He stayed gentle and controlled but pushed himself deeper. His fingers stroked over her clit like he was painting her pleasure back into existence. And slowly, her tension changed. The sharp edges softened. Her moans turned to gasps, her hips rocked into his.

Christian felt the shift and smiled against her skin.

She whimpered, breath stuttering, thighs trembling. "Oh, God . . ."

"That's it," he said again, thrusting deeper, circling her clit faster. "Come for me, Merry. Let go."

She cried out, her body clenching hard around him, as she came for a second time.

"Fuck," Christian groaned, as with one last, desperate thrust, he spilled inside her, body shuddering, lost in the heat and the high and her.

They collapsed forward on to the dresser, skin slick, breath heaving, still connected.

Christian kissed the curve of her spine and whispered, "Told you."

Merry let out a shaky laugh. "You're a menace."

He grinned, pressing another kiss to her damp shoulder and stayed still for a moment, both of them catching their breath, bodies tangled and trembling, hearts still hammering. Then he eased out of her carefully, hands steady on her hips as her knees wobbled.

"I've got you," he whispered.

Merry turned and blinked up at him, dazed and flushed and beautiful. Her lips parted like she wanted to say something, but all that came out was a tiny sigh as her eyes fluttered shut for a beat. He smiled and brushed a damp strand of hair off her cheek.

"You're done standing for the night," he said softly, then bent and scooped her into his arms.

She let out a sleepy, surprised sound as her arms looped around his neck, but she didn't protest. Just curled into him, her head resting on his shoulder, the scent of candy canes rising from her skin.

Christian carried her across to her bed, his bare feet soft against the wooden floor. The storm outside still raged, rain streaking the windows with loud slaps. He reached the bed and eased her down gently on to the cool sheets, pulling the covers up around her neck and making sure she was cocooned. She looked up at him, lashes heavy, eyes soft.

"You okay?" he asked, crouching beside the mattress, brushing his thumb along her jaw.

She nodded, her voice barely a whisper. "Better than okay."

That did something to him. Twisted his chest in that aching, vulnerable way he hadn't expected tonight. He slid into bed beside her, propped on one elbow, the other hand reaching up to stroke her damp hair back from her forehead.

"You're incredible," he murmured. "Just in case no one's told you that recently."

Merry gave him a sleepy smile, her eyes fluttering shut, then opening again, like something had just occurred to her.

"You remember what you said earlier? That you weren't great at impressing women?"

Christian raised a brow. "Yeah . . ."

"Well," she murmured, voice already fading with exhaustion, "I'd say you're actually pretty good at it."

"Is that your official verdict?" He huffed a quiet laugh.

"I told you I'd let you know by midnight."

He leaned in, kissed her temple. "Worth the wait?"

Merry hummed, too tired to answer properly. Christian lay beside her long after she drifted off, watching her chest rise and fall in the dark, his fingers still stroking her hair.

He stayed as long as he dared.

But the clock on her nightstand kept ticking forward, and reality tugged at the edges. His ridiculously early shift at Carroll's would be starting soon, and if he didn't move now, he wouldn't make it back in time.

He eased himself off her bed, careful not to jostle the mattress. Crouching to gather his clothes, he tugged them on piece by piece in the low light. His jacket was still damp, but he shrugged it on, then stood by the bed for a moment longer, watching her before slipping out into the hallway.

The apartment was dark except for the faint blue glow of a phone screen. Merry's roommate was standing there in oversized pyjamas, holding a mug and staring at him with an unimpressed raised brow. He grinned sheepishly, lifting a finger to his lips. Her expression didn't change, but she gave a tiny nod and stepped aside to let him pass. Christian suppressed a laugh and slipped out into the stairwell, pulling the door quietly shut behind him.

Outside, the storm had mostly passed, the streets still shining with rain and glittering under the amber glow of streetlights. He walked to the corner, collar turned up against the cold and raised a hand to flag down a cab. One pulled over almost instantly and he slid into the back seat, giving the driver the address for Carroll's. As the car pulled away from the kerb, he leaned his head back against the seat, the scent of Merry still clinging to his skin, and smiled to himself.

After a few quiet blocks, he pulled out his phone and opened the APEX group chat. It was mostly dead — the guys were probably asleep — but he tapped out a message anyway.

Christian: *Is it okay to pretend to be someone you're not if there's a beautiful woman involved? Asking for a friend.*

He stared at it for a second, then added:

Christian: *@Blake @Nate You two are in different time zones — any moral wisdom from abroad? Or just tell me I'm not a total asshole.*

He hit send, locked the screen, and exhaled. Maybe tonight had been a bad idea. Maybe he should've told her the truth.
His phone buzzed in his lap.

Nate: *Mate. If pretending gets you laid, I'm not judging. Just don't get caught — or do, depending on how good the sex was.*

Christian huffed out a laugh as another buzz sounded from his phone.

Blake: *Depends. Are we talking pretending to like her taste in music or pretending you don't own a billion-dollar brand?*

Christian rolled his eyes, but his grin widened.

Nate: *Tell the truth eventually. But if she's hot and cool she might be worth the risk.*

Blake: *Seconded. You need to be honest with her. And can you give us a description? Or a photo?*

Christian stared at the screen for a beat, thumbs hovering. Then he sent the photo he'd snapped of Merry with her candy cane.

Christian: *I'm in trouble, aren't I?*

The typing dots appeared instantly.

Blake: *Big trouble.*

Nate: *Hot. Mate, if you're not honest with her soon then I'm swooping in and rescuing her from you.*

Christian: *You two are the worst and also may be right. This went further than I meant it to, and now I don't know how to undo it.*

He hit send, then slid his phone back into his jacket pocket just as the cab slowed in front of Carroll's. Christian paid the driver, pulled up his collar against the lingering drizzle, and headed for the staff entrance.

CHAPTER 15

MERRY

Merry slouched through the toy department, too tired to even glance at Santa. She was late again, but this time it had nothing to do with traffic and everything to do with a tall, dark stranger.

"Honestly, if you never see him again, it was still worth it," her roommate had declared over cornflakes that morning. "You look like you've been hit by a truck, in a good way. And that was the hottest sex I've ever heard."

Merry had blushed, bleary-eyed and sore in places that made walking feel oddly theatrical. But as she pulled on her boots in the hallway, trying not to wince, the ache in her body was nothing compared to the one sitting squarely in her chest. Christian was leaving New York. He'd told her that much.

She'd hoped — stupidly, maybe — that he'd change his mind. Or at least say something in daylight that made sense of the way he'd looked at her in the dark. But when she woke up alone, with only a half-drunk glass of water by the bed, she wasn't sure if she'd been something he wanted or just

107

something he needed. Maybe she wasn't supposed to know the difference. Maybe it didn't matter.

As she reached the staff area door, it started to open. Two girls that Merry half knew from the store floor walked out, and when they saw her they burst into giggles. Merry frowned, watching them go and feeling suddenly worried. Had she forgotten to put on trousers? Did she have I-had-hot-sex-last-night written on her face? She patted herself down as she walked into the corridor, but everything seemed to be where it was supposed to be.

Another girl walked past, her cheeks reddening and her mouth curling into a smile as she peeked at Merry. Then a guy passed her, and he too was smirking like she was the butt of some joke.

"What?" Merry said to his back, but her words were too quiet for him to hear.

It felt like one of those nightmares where everybody stares at you and you end up naked. Ahead, the locker room door opened and Alice skipped out, doing her hair as she went. Her eyes widened when she saw Merry, and she pulled the hairpin from between her lips.

"Yes, Merry!" she said, pinning her hair back. "You're here."

"What's going on?" Merry asked. "I feel like I've got, like, a teapot growing out of my head or something."

"Better than that," said Alice, taking Merry's arm and leading her into the locker room. "We've all been trying to guess. Who is it?"

Who is what? she wanted to ask, but she'd suddenly forgotten how to speak.

The large locker room looked exactly the way it had yesterday: lockers down each side for the staff to put their belongings, benches lined up down the middle, a door that led to the restrooms and showers. The only thing that was different was a bouquet of white, pink and red roses sitting on one of the benches. She could smell them from here.

"What are they? Who are they for?"

"Don't play the innocent," Alice said. "They're for you!"

Merry frowned. That was impossible. In her whole life, she had only ever been given flowers once when she was a teenager and her cat had died. Her granny had picked her a bunch of poppies to help her feel better.

"Go on! I can't wait any longer!" She gave Merry a gentle nudge and Merry walked reluctantly to the bench. The flowers really were beautiful, full and proud and shiny. They must have cost a fortune. Nestled among the leaves was a little envelope, her name written on the front in beautiful calligraphy. Merry looked at Alice and Alice urged her on.

"If you don't," her friend said. "I will."

"Oh, fine," Merry said. She plucked the envelope free and opened it, slipping out the little card inside. On the front was a single candy cane, striped red and white. All that was written inside was:

Thanks for last night.

Her cheeks flushed hot and she slid the card back into the envelope with shaking hands, tucking it into her coat pocket like contraband.

"Well, *who*?" squealed Alice, snatching the card. "There's no name! What the hell does 'thanks for last night' mean?"

It didn't need a name. She knew exactly who had sent them — she could still feel the after-effects of being a good girl this morning.

"I swear, I am going to explode if you don't tell me!" Alice said.

"Then you'll have to explode," Merry said. "Because it's nobody, it's nothing. It's . . . ."

Christian was leaving soon for the other side of the world. What did he want from her? A few weeks of hot chocolates and hotter sex and then a sad goodbye? It didn't seem fair that he was playing with her heart like this.

"It's a joke," she said, the smile falling from her face. "A stupid joke. You can have the flowers. I don't want them."

"I think it's the boss," said Trudy from the bench where she was getting changed. 'Lewis Carroll himself. I think that's why you can't say anything."

"Ew!" Merry said, and Alice's laughter was so loud it echoed off the wall.

"That's it!" she said. "That has to be it!"

"No!" said Merry. "That's just wrong. He's like a hundred years old."

"So who, then?" Alice said. "Who would send you a bouquet of flowers like that? From Florisan's, too — they're expensive."

"Come on," said Jasmin. "I mean, you're obviously going to bring him to the Christmas Ball, so you have to tell us who he is before then."

Merry took a deep breath. "Okay, I'm not going to tell you who," she said. "But I'll say *what*."

The three women fell silent with anticipation, and Merry cast a quick look over her shoulder to make sure they were alone.

"So, the other day I was just standing at the door, greeting people, and this guy walks in. He's . . . I mean, he's amazing. He's the most beautiful man I've ever seen."

Merry was blushing so hard she could toast marshmallows on her cheeks. Her three friends listened on, wide-eyed.

"I felt something for him. It's like . . . Okay, this is going to sound really corny, but bear with me. It's like, you know how when you're a kid you make a Christmas wish, and Santa brings it to you. Every single wish is different, and he brings you exactly what you ask for."

"Uh, Merry," said Jasmin in a fake whisper. "I have news. Santa isn't real."

"No, I know," said Merry. "But when you're a kid you think it's magic. It's just your parents, they pick your presents, but in your heart, when you're young, you know it's something else, something incredible. That's how it feels now, with

110

him. I feel like he's a perfect present for me and me alone. He's my Christmas wish come true."

"Wow," said Alice. "So you're dating?"

"That's just it," said Merry. "We're not dating. We're not *anything*. We can't be together."

"Why?" said Trudy. "He sends you flowers, he makes you blush, he's the perfect man."

"But he's going away," said Merry. "He's leaving in a few weeks. He lives in Asia."

"Oh," said Alice, with a genuine expression of sympathy. "That sucks."

Merry shrugged sadly. "It does. I don't even know how I feel about it."

"That's easy," said Alice. "How did you feel when you saw the flowers?"

"Sick," said Merry. "Sick, and shaky, and like my head was about to explode, and happy, but sad, and sick. Did I say I felt sick?"

All three girls laughed.

"Whoa, boy," said Jasmin.

"Hey, ladies!"

Everybody turned to see Diane walking across the room, peeling out of her damp coat.

"You would not believe the day I had yesterday," Diane said, and Merry was infinitely grateful to the woman for taking the attention away from her. "Walker surprised me — he drove me up to Bear Mountain in his Porsche. He brought this picnic with him, and we had it by the river. It was so romantic, and he gave me this."

She flashed the necklace she was wearing and the three women opposite Merry squealed again. It was a beautiful piece of jewellery — woven strands of gold and silver with a teardrop-shaped pendant. The diamond in the middle of it looked the size of Merry's pinky nail.

"Oh, wow," said Jasmin. "That must have cost thousands."

Diane held up both hands, all her slender fingers extended. "Ten. He told me. That's the advantage of having a boyfriend who works on Wall Street." Diane turned to Merry, and the smile on her face was strangely cold. "Speaking of which," she said. "Who do those flowers belong to and where are they from?"

"Merry, and she won't tell," said Alice, pouting. "The spoilsport."

"Oh, won't she?" Diane's eyes glinted like sharpened steel. "Well, I know who it is."

"What?" said Merry. "How?"

"Because my cousin works in a café off Fifth Avenue," Diane said. "And she saw you there two nights ago. She wouldn't have said anything, except she said you were with the most gorgeous man she had ever set eyes on."

Merry's cheeks were practically on fire.

"She said that nobody could take their eyes off him all night. She even took a photo, because she didn't think I'd believe her."

"Show us!" said Jasmin.

"I don't need to," said Diane. "Because he works here."

"I knew it!" said Trudy. "It's Lewis Carroll!"

"Ew," said Diane. "No, not him. It's—"

"Please," said Merry. "I don't want it to—"

"It's one of the janitors," said Diane, with a little laugh that made Merry's blood run cold.

"A *janitor*?" said Alice, frowning. "What?"

"Surely not," said Jasmin, her face wrinkling. "That's just weird."

Merry squirmed in her chair. She felt horribly uncomfortable and she wasn't even sure why. So what if Christian was a janitor? It's a good job, a much-needed job. She didn't care at all what he did for a living — in fact, she admired a man who worked with his hands, who wasn't ashamed to get a little dirty.

But something in the way her friends were staring at her made her feel ashamed, for a reason she couldn't quite put her finger on. Diane had just told them all how her rich boyfriend had driven her out of the city for a romantic picnic before splashing out on a ridiculously expensive necklace. Alice was dating a lawyer and Jasmin had just broken up with a partner in an architecture firm. Merry had heard countless stories of how they had been spoiled and pampered by their men, and the thought of them judging her on her choice of boyfriend made her feel about three inches tall. She felt like she had back at school — backed into a corner until she lied to make the cool kids like her.

"He's not *just* a janitor," she said with a little laugh. She stared at the flowers and clenched her fists, hating herself for what she was about to say — which had nothing to do with how she herself felt about Christian and his career, and everything to do with how her friends felt about *her*. "Why on earth would I date a janitor? No way."

Everyone had fallen quiet, and Merry glanced up to see that nobody was looking at her. They were all staring to the side, their mouths open. Merry's heart actually missed a beat, a wave of dread pouring over her.

Please, she begged, but even before she turned around she knew who she was going to see there.

Christian stood in the open staff room door. He was pale, and his mouth was open as if he had been physically struck. He looked at Merry with glossy eyes, as if he couldn't believe what he'd just heard, then he turned and left the room.

"Oh no!" Merry pushed herself up so fast her chair toppled over behind her.

"He really is hot," said Diane, still smiling.

"Merry, go get him," said Alice, her expression one of deep sympathy. "Go now, before it's too late."

Merry ran through the door, calling Christian's name, and saw his trolley abandoned next to the wall.

It was already too late. He had gone.

CHAPTER 16

CHRISTIAN

Christian pushed through the staff door so hard it slammed against the wall, almost splitting the plaster. He stormed down the corridor, his head spinning, his heart drumming. Behind him he heard Merry's faint voice calling his name, but he didn't turn back.

Her words had hurt. They'd pierced him like a blade and left a gaping wound. How wrong had he been about her? All this time he'd thought she was kind, and sincere, and honest, but in reality she was just like everyone else he'd met since he'd been here. All she cared about was status.

He walked back on to the store floor, losing himself among the shelves of baubles and tinsel. Merry's words echoed in his head — *why on earth would I date a janitor?* — and he felt his blood boil. He wasn't even a janitor, but the fact was that she had judged him based on the job she thought he had. She had belittled him, in front of her friends, and reduced him to a cliché.

But it was a good thing. It made his life so much easier now. He could forget about Merry, focus on the job at hand, find out what was going on in the store, and then get out of New York City before it did any more damage.

He heard the sound of a door behind him and he peered between two dolls to see Merry emerge on to the store floor. She was beside herself, trying to conceal her tears with her hands. But he couldn't let himself feel anything other than anger, despite her upset.

He stayed in the shadows for the rest of his shift, ducking behind the displays whenever Merry appeared. He stalked through the craft goods using his trolley as cover, pretending to check off displays while watching her from a distance. Every now and then she'd falter, a slight pause when she thought nobody was looking, a flicker of pain crossing her face before she straightened her back and smiled again. She looked wrecked — cheeks blotchy, nose red, her usual sparkle dulled to a flicker. Still, she pushed a smile on to her face when she spoke to customers with the kind of forced cheer that made Christian's chest tighten in spite of himself.

His shift ended just after the morning rush and as he was leaving, he saw her crouch down to talk to a little girl who was holding a plush reindeer almost as big as she was. Merry asked the child's name, admired the reindeer, then turned the tag around and said, "Guess what? He's on sale today, but only if you promise to take extra special care of him." The girl beamed, and her mother mouthed *"Thank you"* with a look of quiet relief as Merry took them to the till. Christian looked away, jaw clenched.

Damn her.

Damn her for being kind. For caring when she didn't have to. For proving with every gentle interaction that she wasn't like the others, no matter what she'd said back in the locker room. He should walk away — he didn't know why he was keeping an eye on her in the first place. Instead, he turned down the next aisle to get a better look, and froze.

Just ahead, tucked between a rack of Pop Mart boxes, Margot was whispering furiously to Mrs Cradley. Christian stepped behind an elaborate display of JellyCats and listened.

Margot's voice was low, but he caught fragments between the shouts of overexcited kids and the jingle of a nearby toy display.

". . . It's too much," she said. "I told you this would happen."

Mrs Cradley gave a sharp sniff. "Then we need to stop him. Before he ruins everything."

Christian's heart thudded in his chest. *Stop him?* He leaned closer, trying not to shift the cardboard cutout.

"I'm not sure how long we can keep covering for him," Margot said. "If he keeps snooping—"

Cradley glanced around. "He's poking around in places he shouldn't. If we don't get ahead of this, it could all come undone."

Christian's fists clenched. *They're talking about me. They know I've been looking into the sales anomalies.*

Mrs Cradley adjusted her clipboard with a sigh. "I've got to get upstairs. Just . . . keep him busy, will you? And don't let him near the other Carroll."

Margot nodded. "I'll handle it."

They parted quickly. Cradley disappearing towards the staff elevator, and Margot vanishing down the aisle. Christian stayed hidden a moment longer, heart racing, trying to piece it all together.

He knows too much . . . Stop him . . . Keep him busy . . .

So they were hiding something. He wasn't paranoid after all. Christian backed away slowly, slipping into the board games aisle and leaning against a stack of Guess Who. Something was definitely going on and it sounded like he was running out of time to find out what.

Merry had done him a favour. Without her as a distraction he could concentrate all his efforts on saving Carroll's, which is what he should have been doing all along. He desperately needed to do some more research and he was also desperately in need of a shower so he decided to head back to his hotel and sort out both.

Christian dropped off his trolley and stepped out into the brittle winter sunlight, the city wind whipping down Fifth Avenue with no regard for his mood. He tightened his coat and kept his head down, ignoring the smell of roasting chestnuts from a nearby vendor, the twinkle of lights in the plaza tree, the sound of tourists cooing over store windows. Last night, Christmas in New York had been magic. Right now, it felt like a bad joke.

His hotel was just over the road and he smiled at the doorman as he ducked inside. A grand chandelier glittered overhead and the floors gleamed like a freshly frozen pond, but none of that mattered to him as he hurried to the elevator and hit the button to call it to take him up to his penthouse suite.

It was more apartment than hotel room: double-height ceilings, floor-to-ceiling windows that overlooked the park, and a Christmas tree so tastefully decorated it looked like it belonged in a lifestyle magazine. Christian didn't bother turning on the lights. He let the winter daylight filter in through the glass, casting everything in that same cold grey that had settled over him too.

He dropped his bag by the sofa and pulled off his coat, remembering that Merry still had his lumberjack jacket. That was probably lost to him now, too, much the same as she was, which was a shame as they had been both turning into his favourites. He walked through the suite, stripping off his jumper, unbuttoning his shirt, tugging loose the rest as he made his way to the en suite bathroom.

Steam billowed quickly in the glass-and-marble shower, fogging the mirrors and softening the edges of the room. Christian stepped under the hot spray, bracing his hands against the tiled wall as the water sluiced over him. For a while, he just stood there, letting it beat down on his shoulders, willing it to scald away the confusion and the pain, and the way her voice still echoed in his ears.

But it was no use. Because the second he closed his eyes, she was there.

The memory of Merry hit him like hot treacle. The scent of her skin, the press of her mouth, the way her breath had caught when he'd kissed down her throat. He could feel the silk of her thighs against his hands, the tremble in her legs when he made her come, the taste of her still on his tongue.

He pressed his forehead to the cool tile and drew breath. And then the sweetness turned sour. *Why on earth would I date a janitor?* The pain sliced through him, a punch straight to his gut from the betrayal he hadn't seen coming.

He slammed his palm against the wall, the sound echoing in the marble room. This wasn't supposed to happen. He wasn't supposed to feel anything. But somehow, Merry had gotten under his skin, past his defences, and she hadn't even known who he really was. Maybe that was the cruellest part of all.

He scrubbed a hand down his face, trying to wash her out of his system. With a grunt, he forced himself upright and finished showering quickly, the sting of the hot water turning lukewarm by the time he shut it off.

He stepped out, wrapped a thick white towel around his waist and ran a hand through his dripping hair as he padded barefoot into the living area. The floor-to-ceiling windows threw long stripes of winter light across the rug and, in the sudden hush, the city felt a million miles away.

The folder from his dad sat where he'd left it on the coffee table and Christian dropped on to the sofa and spread the papers out in front of him. Financials, staff rotas, delivery logs, anonymised internal complaints. He scanned the pages, eyes flicking from margin to margin, looking for gaps, overlaps, irregularities. Anything that would point the finger at Margot and maybe Mrs Cradley, the Dragon Lady, too.

But his concentration was splintered. His body ached, and not just from the manual labour of work over the last few days. A deep, bone-level tiredness tugged at him. He made it halfway through the second delivery report before his eyelids started to droop. He shifted, blinked hard, and tried again. Then suddenly he was gone.

The city kept moving outside the glass, horns and sirens, and wind against the panes. But inside the penthouse suite, Christian slumped sideways on the couch, towel askew, papers scattered around him like snowdrifts. And in sleep, his brow was furrowed, because even in his dreams, Merry was still there.

CHAPTER 17

MERRY

The store was finally empty. The last customer had left nearly forty minutes ago, arms loaded with snow globes and scented candles. Now the aisles were quiet, the lights dimmed to their evening setting, and only a few of the closing team remained, straightening shelves and sweeping glitter into neat little piles.

Merry stood in the staff room, rubbing at the base of her spine. Her feet were killing her. Her head throbbed, her throat hurt from forcing a smile all day, and her eyes stung with unshed tears.

She was two hours past the end of her shift and she really should have gone home, but the chaos of the holiday rush had swallowed the day whole, and she'd barely noticed the time ticking by. It was only now, as she was peeling off her uniform and looking at the clock, that it hit her how exhausted she was. And how hollow she felt.

Christian hadn't come back. Not that she could blame him. He'd disappeared into the store and hadn't resurfaced, and it had taken everything in her not to cry openly every time she remembered the look of betrayal in his eyes.

Her words had hurt him. Worse, they'd changed how he saw her, and she deserved that. But she wasn't that person, and now she'd have no way to tell him how sorry she was.

Pulling her coat tightly around herself, Merry trudged towards the exit, her boots squeaking against the polished floor. She braced herself, ready to face the cold, then stopped. Across the empty shop floor, she caught sight of a familiar shape in jeans and a thick sweater, his damp hair curling slightly at the ends. Christian.

She froze, caught somewhere between relief and panic. He didn't look like he was on shift — he wasn't in his overalls and his trolley was nowhere to be seen — and from what Merry had seen on her stalk of the rota, he wasn't due on again until the morning. What was he doing back?

She stayed hidden for a moment, half in shadow by the display of discounted snow globes. But she couldn't look away. The sight of him clean-shaven, freshly showered, hit her like a sucker punch.

He moved towards the staff elevators, glancing over his shoulder once before stepping inside. Without thinking, Merry launched into a sprint. She darted past the checkout into the lobby and pressed the button just as Christian's elevator was heading upwards. She had no idea where he was going so she jabbed all the buttons in the hope she'd not lose him.

The elevator doors opened on all the floors but there was no one to be seen. She shifted from foot to foot, nerves jangling, heart pounding in her throat. By floor seven, she was sure she'd lost him. And then, as the elevator slowed again and the doors slid open on ten, she saw him.

He was just ahead, walking past a stack of unopened toy crates ready for the night staff to restock the shelves, his broad shoulders hunched, hands shoved into the pockets of his jeans. Merry held her breath in the hope he hadn't seen her. She stepped out quietly, letting the doors whisper shut behind her, and followed at a distance as he weaved through the shadowy shelves making for the staff corridor.

Hurrying in behind him, she watched as he reached a door she'd never noticed before — unmarked, tucked between two dusty filing cabinets — and slipped through. She hesitated for the briefest moment, then followed him.

The rooftop wind hit her like an icy slap. She ducked her head and kept going, following the sound of his footsteps on the gravel. He was heading across the roof, weaving between battered storage units and rusting vents. She stayed low, trailing him from a distance, boots crunching softly against the frost-dusted path to a strange building ahead.

Tucked right into the northwest corner of the roof, it looked almost like a conservatory or an old orangery, its structure domed and delicate, entirely made of glass with ornate cast-iron supports painted white. Inside was a forest of green ferns and palms and vines pressing against the glass, like they were trying to burst free. Merry's jaw dropped at the idea there was a whole ecosystem living on the roof of Carroll's.

Christian reached the door and paused.

"You'd make an awful spy," he said, his voice carrying on the wind across the rooftop to her.

Her cheeks burned. She straightened up, pulling her coat tighter and forcing herself forward. "I-I'm sorry," she blurted out as she reached him. "Christian, I'm so sorry about what I said. I didn't mean it. I'm not. . . God, I'm just so—"

But he held up a hand and stopped her in her tracks.

"Come inside," he said. "It's freezing, and if we're going to do this, I'd rather not lose a foot to frostbite in the interim."

Merry nodded, swallowing hard. She followed him as he opened the glass-panelled door and stepped into the conservatory. The change in temperature was immediate. The air was warm and slightly humid, scented with greenery and soil.

It was like stepping into another world. Merry was surprised at how big it was, and how well looked after. Three of the four walls were almost entirely covered with potted plants, making the space feel like a jungle. She was studying it so intently that she didn't even notice the fourth wall until Christian pointed to it.

"How's that for a view?" he said.

Through the glass Merry could see Fifth Avenue before her, almost as far as the park. Cars busied themselves on the road, their horns soft and muted, and tiny people crowded the street. The world down there was alive with lights, the storefronts glowing with illuminated snowflakes, fountains of colour pouring down from the rooftops, one store wrapped in a Santa's belt of snowy bulbs and a giant snowman dancing on another.

Christian moved deeper inside, stopping beside an old leather sofa near the back. A matching easy chair sat opposite, flanked by a small wooden table stacked with gardening books and a half-used candle.

"Sit," he said softly.

She lowered herself into the armchair. It was incredibly comfortable, moulding itself to her body, and she laid a blanket over her legs, less to keep her warm and more to shield herself. Christian sat on the sofa, leaning forward and massaging his stubble with one hand. He looked like he was trying to figure out what to say, and she leaped in before he could start.

"I need to say this," Merry said, trying to be brave. "And I need you to let me finish, even if it's awful."

Christian's eyes didn't catch hers, but he gave a small nod, his expression unreadable.

"I'm so sorry," she began. "What I said in the locker room . . . I can't take it back, and I wouldn't blame you if you never wanted to speak to me again. But please know, I didn't mean it. Not really. Not the way it came out."

She clenched her hands in her lap, twisting the edge of the soft blanket between her fingers.

"I don't know what happened. One second I was defending you, and the next . . . it was like I was thirteen again. Back at school. Back in that horrible corridor where the rich girls would laugh at me because my dad showed up in his gardening gear to pick me up. Where they'd point out his cracked hands, his scuffed boots, and say things loud enough for me to hear."

She glanced away, eyes fixed on the glass walls and the glittering city beyond.

"They called him all sorts of names, like he wasn't a person who worked every hour he could, just to keep us afloat with my sister's hospital bills. We were broke. And I never cared — until those girls made me feel like I should. Until I learned that kindness and sacrifice meant nothing if you didn't have the right shoes or bag or white-collar job."

Christian still said nothing and Merry wanted to cry at the hurt on his face and the way he still wouldn't look at her.

"I said something cruel because I was scared," she admitted. "But these last couple of days you've made me feel something I haven't felt in years. You've made me feel wanted. And then I panicked. Because you're leaving and I'm going to be stuck with those girls for eternity. So I picked them. And I'm sorry." Her voice broke, and she pressed a hand to her chest. "You're the first person I've trusted in a long time. And when you looked at me like you didn't know who I was anymore . . . I deserved it. I did. But I want you to know something."

Christian finally met her gaze.

"I don't care what you do for a living. You could sweep floors or own the building, because it's not your job that matters. It's you. You're a better man than anyone I've ever met." She drew a shaky breath the words spilling out faster now. "You're kind. You listen. You make people feel like they matter. You made me feel like I matter. And if I've ruined it, I'll live with that. But I needed to tell you the truth before you leave. You are enough just as you are."

Silence settled over them again, as thick as the vines that curled around the glass above. Merry sat perfectly still, her hands clenched in her lap, her heart full of regret and hope — and she wasn't sure which was the more painful of the two.

Christian didn't speak for a long time. Then he let out a slow breath and leaned back slightly, his eyes never leaving hers.

"You did hurt me," he said quietly. "I'm not going to pretend you didn't. Hearing you say that . . . it knocked the wind out of me."

Merry's heart crumpled. She opened her mouth, but he held up a hand.

"But," he said, his voice softer, "I understand what you're saying. I've been there, too, saying things you don't mean because you're scared or backed into a corner. I get it." He looked down for a second, then back up at her, brow creased. "And the truth is . . . I believe you. I believe you didn't mean it."

Relief swelled so quickly in Merry's chest it almost hurt.

Christian gave her the faintest, crooked smile. "I know what it's like to be judged before someone knows who you are. I've spent most of my life trying to figure out who sees me for me, and who just sees the money — you know, the lack of it. When I met you, I thought you saw me."

"I did," she said quickly. "I do."

"I know," he said.

Merry gave a shaky smile. "So . . . friends?"

His mouth twitched. "Friends?" he echoed, standing slowly and stepping closer, holding out his hands to her. "I don't think I can do just friends."

Her breath caught as he reached down and took her hand, tugging gently until she rose from the chair, the blanket sliding to the floor.

"I know I shouldn't be doing this," he whispered, his mouth inches from hers. "I'm leaving. I'm supposed to keep my distance. But I can't." His fingers brushed her cheek. "I can't help myself."

Then he kissed her softly. His hands slid into her hair, drawing her closer, his body pressed to hers, and Merry melted into it with relief. She clutched the front of his sweater, kissed him with everything she'd been holding back. His tongue traced hers and she gasped, heat flooding her belly as he backed her gently towards the sofa, his hands skimming down her arms, her waist, until she bumped into the edge and sat down.

"What you said to me about being enough," he said. "I want you to know that the same applies to you. You don't have to shrink yourself or be afraid of what people think."

Merry stared up at him, heart pounding.

"You're enough, Merry," he murmured, brushing his knuckles along her jaw. "Exactly as you are."

Her eyes filled. "Christian . . ."

He leaned in again, pressing a kiss to the corner of her mouth. Then her cheek. Her jaw. Down, down . . . until his mouth found her throat, her pulse fluttering wildly beneath his lips. Her breath caught as he dropped to his knees between her thighs, lifting the hem of her uniform with warm, deliberate hands and gently peeling down her tights. The cool air kissed her skin as he looked up at her from the floor, eyes dark with heat, expression full of reverence. "And I'm going to show you."

She paused, breathless. "Wait. Christian, are you sure no one's going to come in? What is this place, how did you find it?"

He leaned back slightly, still kneeling, his hands resting gently on her thighs. "I found it the other day when I was cleaning the roof," he said, a smile tugging at his mouth. "I spotted the door and figured it was just storage, but when I opened it, this was all here. Totally abandoned, but someone's clearly still tending to it. There's a watering can tucked under those books, and the soil's fresh in half the pots."

"What if someone comes?" she murmured, lost in the way his fingers were stroking her thighs.

"You," he said, eyes returning to hers with a wicked glint. "That'll just be you."

His hands slid higher, warming her skin as he gently parted her thighs. Then he kissed her through her knickers. A warm press of his mouth that made her hips jerk and a soft gasp escape her lips.

"Christian . . ."

She barely got the word out before he did it again, this time dragging his tongue slowly along the damp cotton, teasing her through it, making her knees tremble.

"You're already wet for me," he murmured, like it was the most beautiful thing he'd ever discovered.

Then he slipped his fingers beneath the edge of her knickers and drew them aside, exposing her to the humid air and his hungry gaze. She sucked in a breath as he looked at her like he'd been starving and finally found something worth feasting on. He leaned in and kissed her bare skin, open-mouthed and slow, then flattened his tongue and licked a long, deliberate stroke from the bottom of her slit to the top. Merry cried out softly, her head tipping back, her hands flying to his hair.

Then he did it again. And again. Until her breath was catching, her hips rolling forward instinctively, chasing the rhythm he was building. When he sucked her clit into his mouth her whole body lit up.

A whimper escaped her. "Oh my God."

He groaned against her, the sound vibrating through her, and slipped one hand lower, two fingers gliding easily into her slick heat. He filled her slowly, drawing them back out, then sliding in again, matching the tempo of his tongue.

Her body was on fire. Every nerve ending sparking to life, every part of her straining towards him, held together only by the grip of his hands and the heat of his mouth. It was overwhelming. It was perfect.

He alternated the pressure on her clit, circling it with his tongue, then sucking it between his lips again while his fingers moved inside her, finding that spot that made her legs tremble and her cries catch in her throat. She was so close.

"Don't stop," she whispered, breathless. "Please, don't stop."

He didn't. He just kept going, worshipping her with every stroke and every kiss, until she came in a release that washed over her like a wave. She cried out his name, her thighs clamping around his shoulders as she bucked beneath him, all control lost.

When he finally pulled back, her knickers still askew and her chest rising and falling like she'd run a marathon, he looked up at her with a flushed face and a crooked, satisfied grin.

"You are more than enough," he said, voice rough with emotion. "Don't ever forget that."

Merry could barely move, which is why it was Christian who bolted to his feet at the sound of crunching gravel outside the conservatory.

"Shit!" he said, looking at Merry in wide-eyed alarm. "Quick."

Merry launched herself out of the sofa and glanced through the wall of foliage. "Shit," she agreed, unable to believe her eyes as Mrs Cradley strode towards the conservatory. "She must have a sixth sense."

"Or some kind of fun-destroying radar," said Christian, tugging at his trousers. "Come on, let's get out of here."

She grabbed her tights and slipped her shoes on and they sneaked out through the conservatory door, running for a large vent. They hid behind it, watching as Mrs Cradley walked into the conservatory and closed the door behind her.

Together, hissing with barely contained laughter, they ran the long way around the roof, making their way back to the door and tumbled inside.

CHAPTER 18

CHRISTIAN

The last thing Christian wanted to do was head back to his room. He'd come out for a reason after waking from his nap, still groggy, heart pounding from a half-remembered dream. He was pretty sure Mrs Cradley was hiding something. The rooftop conservatory wasn't listed on any staff floor plan, and he'd caught her sneaking out the door a few times. So, he'd come to poke around. Only, halfway across the gravel, he'd felt that unmistakable prickle between his shoulder blades that told him he was being followed. The last person he'd expected it to be was Merry.

She'd followed him. Apologised. Said all the things he hadn't let himself hope she might say. And now she'd gone, and he was wired. Still tasting her on his lips and burning with the memory of her hands in his hair. They'd barely touched the surface of what he wanted to do to her when Mrs Cradley had appeared like a Victorian ghost with a sixth sense for sniffing out joy.

Christian figured he'd do a bit of work while he was here — burn off the restlessness that pulsed just beneath his skin.

And if he happened to poke around a little more in the process? Well, there was no harm in that.

He had walked with Merry to the ground floor and kissed her goodbye at the staff door, then made his way back down the corridor and out into the atrium. It was like coming home for the first time in years, the store utterly empty and completely silent. He'd loved these moments when he was a kid, the quiet after the storm when the doors had been locked. He'd had the whole building to himself — well, him and the cleaning crews — and he d explored to his heart's content, playing cowboys and bandits among the hats, sliding hockey pucks along the smooth floors of the sports department, watching the huge TVs in Electronics. He may have been an only child, but the store had been like a sibling to him. It had never let him get lonely.

Now, though, something felt wrong.

Christian walked across the vast, empty atrium. The escalators were still, the lights dimmed. Mannequins stared at him with smiles on their faces. The tree stood before him, smaller than the one at Rockefeller but no less impressive. Hundreds of presents lay around its base, perfectly wrapped and gloriously shiny. Once, when he'd been about four, Christian had opened a dozen or so of them, believing that he would find presents inside. His dad had torn strips off him in anger, but his mum had gathered him in a huge hug and told him it was okay. The next year, he remembered, she'd wrapped a special gift for him and hidden it among the fake presents. She'd done the same the year after, too, and the year after that, helping him find it without causing any damage. She'd promised to do it every single year, but of course she hadn't — later that year she'd gone into hospital and never came home.

He wondered if there would be a present there for him now.

Shaking his head sadly, Christian surveyed the rest of the atrium. It was a mess. Clothes hung off the rails, the floor felt sticky, and the cashier's desks were cluttered and untidy. It was almost like everyone had left at once, midway through their shift, leaving the store like the sailors on the *Mary Celeste*. That was weird. His dad might have been lenient in some ways, but he'd always insisted on the store being spotless before everyone left, ready to open up the next day. Why hadn't anyone bothered? Where was the cleaning team?

Christian rode the customer elevator back up to the tenth floor. It was just as messy up here, Santa's grotto littered with candy wrappers and unclaimed presents. He made his way to the staff door and let himself through, peeking his head around the locker room door to see a man sitting there, lacing up his boots.

"Harvey?" he said.

The man clamped a hand to his heart, wheezing in a breath. "Argh! Christian! Are you trying to send me to my grave? You scared the life outta me."

"Sorry," Christian said, walking into the room. "I didn't think anyone was here."

"That makes two of us," said Harvey, massaging his chest. "I thought you was on an early today? What you doing here?"

"I . . . I just stopped by, thought I'd left my wallet," he said, hating the fact he had to lie. "Where is everyone?"

"Gone."

"But why? I thought Da—" He caught himself just in time. "I thought *Lewis* wanted the store cleaned at the end of every day?"

"They've not gone home for the day," said Harvey. "They've *gone*. Like, for good."

"What?" Christian sat down opposite the man. "Why?"

Harvey shrugged, struggling with his other boot.

"That's half our janitors gone in the last two months," he said. "Not to mention the floor staff. I don't know what's going on, but I can tell you something."

"Yeah?" Christian leaned in.

"Yeah," said Harvey. "I was walking my dog the other night and I bumped into Fred. He was one of the janitors who left. He was climbing into a brand-new Corvette — you know, not *brand* new, but new to him. Wouldn't tell me how he got the money to buy it, but he did say he's not the only one from Carroll's who's suddenly found himself with some extra cash. Told me that if I was patient, I'd get a bonus too."

"A bonus?" Christian asked. "That doesn't make any sense. Why would he get a bonus if he wasn't staying? Were they trying to keep him on?"

"That's just it," said Harvey. "I don't think he got paid to stay, I think he got paid to leave. I think they all did, all the staff who've left, all the janitors. Something strange is going on."

"Yeah," said Christian, frowning. "Something *really* strange."

Harvey struggled up and Christian rushed over to help him.

"Thanks, kiddo," the older man said. "I'm getting too old for this. I did the best I can, but I can't clean the store by myself."

"You did good," Christian said. "Thank you."

He watched Harvey shuffle away, the man's words circling his head like vultures. Why were people being paid to leave the store? And who was paying them? It sounded like deliberate sabotage, and he would bet his bottom dollar that Margot and Mrs Cradley were the reason why.

CHAPTER 19

MERRY

It was the cold that woke Merry. She shivered, pulling the duvet over her head and wondering whether she could get away with spending the whole day in bed. Sadly, the answer was no. She peeked up over her quilts to see that it was a quarter past seven. Her shift started in less than two hours, and it was always a nightmare getting across town in the morning.

Groaning, and bracing herself for the freezing temperatures of her apartment, she threw back the quilts and dashed for the bathroom. She leaped into the shower, turning the water as high as it would go and blasting the chill out of her bones. Gradually, the events of the previous day settled into her waking mind — the flowers, the awful moment in the staff room where she thought she had lost Christian for good, then the rooftop, and the sex, and Mrs Cradley's awful timing.

She snorted into the water at the memory of Christian running as best he could, given the circumstances going on in his jeans. Even with the awkwardness of almost being caught, she wouldn't trade that rooftop moment for anything. She was going to enjoy whatever time she had with him and not get too attached.

Urgh, who was she kidding?

Merry rinsed her hair then drenched it with conditioner. She was frightened to turn the water off because it would be so cold in the bathroom, but she didn't have a choice. She'd got home last night to another two bills with *PAST DUE* emblazoned on the envelopes. If she didn't do something quickly, then she'd lose her heating altogether — and just in time for Christmas.

A feeling of despair opened up inside her like a big, black hole, and she had to fight from falling into it. She wasn't sure how it had got this bad. She'd been working hard all year, and while the pay at Carroll's wasn't amazing, she'd been doing a lot of hours and should have had enough to survive on. But everything was so expensive in New York, and after her rent and utilities, not to mention the money she sent back to help her folks with her sister's bills, she was left with practically nothing. If her dad knew how poor she really was, he would send the money right back to her. But he struggled to find work these days, especially now that he was older. Merry was the only hope they had.

Besides, she was young. She could handle the cold, and she knew it wouldn't be for ever.

Well, she *hoped* it wouldn't be for ever.

She shut off the water and hopped out, drying herself in record time and bundling herself into her jeans, then two sweaters, and an extra pair of socks. She fixed her hair the best she could, then slung on Christian's jacket — with a quick sniff of the collar — and ran for the subway. The city was busier than ever, despite the weather — freezing cold rain lashing itself against the streets, buildings and anyone brave enough to be outside — and by the time Merry ran through the door, dripping on the carpet, it was already ten past nine.

"I'm late!" she said to Diane, who was on greeter duty. She hurried past, but Diane called her back.

"Did you manage to fix things with that guy?" she said. "The janitor? I can't believe you said that!"

Merry's stomach lurched uncomfortably as she recalled the awful moment. "I think so," she said, a grin tugging at her lips as she remembered what had happened afterwards. "I'm pretty sure he's not angry at me. We made up, you know? Anyway we're not really . . . I mean, nothing's really happening. Gotta run, D."

She dashed up to the tenth floor, running to the locker room so fast she almost bowled over the figure who was standing in front of the door.

"Oh, sorry!" she shouted, her heart plummeting into her boots as she recognised Mrs Cradley.

"Miss Sinclair!" Mrs Cradley screeched. "I was waiting for you. Do you know what time it is?"

"I know, I'm so sorry," she said. "It's the traffic. The city is insanely busy."

"Then leave earlier," Dragon Lady said, jabbing a finger at Merry. "This is the third time this week you've been late. It is unacceptable. If you are late one more time, then it will be the final time. Am I making myself clear?"

Merry nodded.

"I said, am I making myself clear?" Mrs Cradley said. "If this job is not valuable to you, I will find somebody else who values it."

"It's clear," said Merry. "Crystal clear. Please, I need this job. I'm sorry, it won't happen again."

The last few words came out alongside a choked sob, and for a moment Mrs Cradley's expression softened. "This store is like a body," she said. "If one part of it stops working, the entire organism stops working. You are a mere cell in this complicated biology, Miss Sinclair, but you are as important as any other. We are so short-staffed that the organism is in danger of failing. If it wasn't for the valiant efforts of the cleaning crew then we wouldn't even have been able to open this morning. So let me ask you again, do you value your position here? Will you do everything you can to keep this store alive?"

"Yes," said Merry. "Yes I will."

Mrs Cradley nodded, then turned sharply and walked off down the corridor.

Smile, Merry! she ordered herself. *And remember, you are an important cell in the organism that is Carroll's Department Store!*

At least the day can't get any worse, she thought as she marched into the locker room — and came face to face with Christian.

"Hey!" he said. He was standing there with his trolley and mop, and he looked exhausted. In fact, she couldn't remember a time in her life when she'd seen anyone look so tired. Still, when he smiled it seemed to light up the whole room. "How are you?"

"Oh, I'm fine," she said, smiling back. However awkwardly the night had ended yesterday, she was always pleased to see him. She could still feel his strong arms around her, could still taste his lips on hers, and the thought of it made her blush. "I'm fine," she said again. "Are you?"

"Yeah," he said, stifling a yawn. He really did look tired, and his clothes were wrinkled and stained. What had Mrs Cradley said about the cleaning crew's valiant effort?

"Are you sure?" she asked. "You look like you worked all night, then slept on the floor of the grotto."

Christian laughed, rubbing the back of his neck. "Just had trouble sleeping."

"Too frustrated?" she asked, a rush of a giggle bursting in her chest. "We can blame Mrs Cradley for that. Who knows what might have happened if she hadn't turned up?"

"Oh, I do."

Merry hid her face in the damp collar of her jacket as her cheeks burned.

Christian put a hand on her sleeve and stepped a bit closer. "This coat is never going to smell the same ever again," he said. "Not that I'm complaining."

"Mm, you definitely weren't complaining last night." She tilted her head up. "Until we got interrupted."

He gripped her chin between his thumb and fingers and dipped in for a kiss. "Don't worry. We can finish what we started another time."

"Promises, promises," she said, into his mouth. "Your turn next time." She stepped back and gave him a cheeky wink.

Christian's eyes darkened. "I'm holding you to that." He cleared his throat and huffed out a breath just as the locker room door opened and a gaggle of canteen staff came bustling in.

"I'll see you around then," Merry called, busying herself with the day's rota tacked to the noticeboard. She was on Jewellery again, which meant another day of irritated customers telling her how useless she was — not to mention the chance of the unhappy couple appearing again to torment her. "And swing by with your mop if you see anyone who needs reminding that we're only human."

Christian barked out a laugh and started pushing his trolley out the door. He faltered, looking back over his shoulder. "Merry," he called. "Would you like to go to the Christmas Carroll Ball with me?"

She froze, her heart doing an actual somersault in her chest. The ball was tomorrow night. She'd heard Diane and the others talking about it non-stop since she started working there — floor-length gowns, champagne towers, fairy lights strung across the chandeliers. It was the kind of thing she'd always dreamed of but never actually believed she'd attend. Especially not on the arm of someone like Christian.

Her first instinct was to say yes. She wanted to go so badly it hurt. But then reality came crashing in — her bank balance was non-existent, the overdraft already groaning, and her single black dress with the broken zip was balled up somewhere at the back of the wardrobe. Even if she somehow scraped together enough for a ticket, what would she wear?

Her smile faltered.

"I—" she started, then stopped. "That's really sweet of you, but I don't know if I can."

Christian frowned, halfway through the door. "Why not?"

She shrugged, trying to keep it breezy. "I'm working a lot of shifts, and it's formal, right? Gowns and tuxedos and whatever? I'm not sure I have anything that fits the brief."

"We don't have to make a big deal of it," he said gently. "I just want to go with you, that's all."

She smiled again, softer this time. "Can I think about it?"

He nodded once, the corner of his mouth quirking. "Of course. But for the record, you'd be the best-dressed person there, even if you came in jeans and your Christmas jumper. And if you do, then I promise to come in my overalls to make you feel less conspicuous."

"I literally don't know what I've done to deserve someone like you in my corner," she said, and it was true. "Thank you. Look, I'd better get changed. I've already been told off once today, and you never know where Mrs Cradley is going to appear next."

"Don't we know it?" said Christian in a hushed voice. "She's like a ninja."

"A dragon ninja," said Merry, watching the door close behind Christian with a smile, wondering if his sprinkling of Christmas magic might just be rubbing off on her.

CHAPTER 20

CHRISTIAN

He grinned all the way to the janitorial office, and it was about the only thing keeping him awake. He had barely slept at all last night, and not just because he'd been thinking about what he'd have liked to carry on doing with Merry before they were rudely interrupted. No, he'd been so distressed at the sight of the store that he'd started cleaning. At first, he was only planning to do the entrance and the atrium, so that at least it looked presentable in the morning. But then he'd spread out into the wings, vacuuming the carpets and polishing the cabinets, filling rubbish bags with the odds and ends he found lying around. He'd straightened the clothes in all the departments and even fluffed the cushions in Homeware. He'd managed to grab a quick nap in the locker room at around 4 a.m., but he'd woken two hours later feeling worse than he had before he'd gone to sleep.

It was a ridiculous thing to do, he knew. It wasn't his job to single-handedly clean the whole store, even if he was a janitor. But part of him still loved this place. He'd spent his whole childhood here, pretty much. It was more a home to him than the huge townhouse they'd owned in the Upper East Side. It had made him unfathomably sad to see it so trashed.

It had got him thinking, too, about why he had stayed here. His dad had asked him to solve the mystery of what was going wrong in the store, and while he wasn't overly keen on doing anything for his father, he understood that he was doing it for the store itself. And he *would* find out what was going wrong. He was getting close already.

Yawning again, he emptied his bucket, cleaned his mop, and refilled his bottles and sprays. He'd head back out in a moment and carry on his shift, but he wanted to report back to his dad first. Splashing some water on his face, he made his way through the staff corridors and past the busy clerks until he reached Lewis Carroll's office. Knocking twice, he opened the door.

Margot was sitting in his father's chair, dwarfed by his immense desk. She looked up from a pile of paperwork, swinging the chair from side to side. She looked way too comfortable there, and the smug look she threw at Christian made it very clear she knew what he was thinking. His dad was nowhere to be seen.

"Margot," he said. "Where's Dad?"

"Christian," she spat back. "He's at home. He wasn't up to coming in today."

The words hit him like a physical blow. He couldn't remember a single time when his dad had been too ill to work. When he'd been a kid he'd prayed sometimes that his dad would get a cold or sprain his ankle, just so that he would stay home and spend time with him.

He walked into the office and closed the door behind him. "What are you doing in here?"

"My job," she replied, looking him up and down. "Shouldn't you be doing yours? I saw the security feed from last night. You're pretty good with a mop. If you like, I can make your janitorial position permanent."

Christian ignored the bait, walking to the other side of the desk. He would not let her intimidate him.

"I am good at my job," he said. "I've learned a lot since I've been here."

"Yeah?" she said. "Like what?"

"Like the fact that people are leaving Carroll's in droves," he said. "The store is half empty, there aren't enough staff."

"We've lost the occasional employee," said Margot. "But it's nothing to worry about. The ones who are left will just have to work twice as hard. In the end, it costs us less."

"It's costing us business," he said. "Customers are leaving."

"It's nothing to do with you," she said. "I'm handling it."

"Are you?" He put his hands on the desk. "Do you know that somebody is paying our staff to leave? Somebody is deliberately sabotaging the store."

Margot smiled coldly. "That's what you think?"

"I don't just think it," he said. "I know it. Somebody is giving cash payouts to anyone who leaves. Somebody wants this business to die."

Margot leaned back, chewing her pen. "So it's another store," she said. "It has to be. Another company is trying to put us under before Christmas. They know that if we don't survive the last quarter, then we're going to be in trouble. Who told you this?"

"A source," said Christian. "You don't need to know."

"I do need to know," said Margot, pushing herself to her feet. "It's my job to know. I'm the only one who can save this company. I'll find out the truth, and when I do, you can pack your things and leave because it will be me sitting at this desk, permanently."

She gave him one of her death stares, and there was something in it that made him instantly suspicious. What had she just said? *I'm the only one who can save this company.*

It was no secret that he hated Margot, but was she really capable of sabotaging Carroll's? Maybe she was trying to make things look bad so that she could fix them, proving to his dad that she had what it took to take over. Or maybe she was being paid off by another store to take out the competition. Carroll's

141

was a big fish — if it sank then it would make room in the pond for a lot of smaller fish to thrive.

"My dad trusts you," said Christian. "I'm not sure he should. I know how ruthless you are, Margot."

"Poor Christian," she said, pouting. "I know deep down you're still desperate for Daddy's approval."

She walked around the desk, standing in front of him and brushing some dust from his overalls.

"I'm not sure if you ever knew this," she went on, "but it was your father who brought me in to toughen you up a bit. He thought I might rub off on you. In his words, you were 'too soft'. All these idealistic notions of fair wages and ethical product lines — very noble and totally naive. Very bad for business."

"What?" said Christian. "That's ridiculous."

"Is it?" she went on, smiling smugly. "He thought you were weak, that you weren't strong enough to run a business like this. Your kindness, my determination. It would be a perfect match. But then I realised you were weak. All those trips overseas to check on the welfare of the factory workers, all those campaigns to pay workers more and treat them better. You cost the store money, and I realised you were a lost cause. You can't teach someone how to have a backbone, Christian. You've either got it or you haven't. Which is why I paid the suppliers in Rapu-Rapu to ask you to stay out there and help them. And they jumped at the chance. As did you."

What? Christian felt sick. He thought he'd been brave getting away from the company, but all this time it had been Margot's wish to get rid of him.

"And I'm glad you did," he said, trying to hide his hurt. "I could never stand your greed. It made me sick. Not everything is about money."

"Says the billionaire," she said.

"It was never about the money for me. But I see you're still obsessed with being rich, being powerful. Is that why you're doing it?"

"Doing what?" she said.

"Paying people to leave," he went on. "I think it's you. I think you're so desperate to take over the company when Dad leaves that you're deliberately sabotaging it. I think you want to march in and fix it, then you'll be the next CEO of the Carroll empire."

Margot chewed over his words for a moment, then she smiled. "Prove it."

She walked away, opening the door and pausing for a moment. "I've worked too hard for this," she said. "You don't get to come back here after five years and take it away from me. I'm going to tell you something, so listen well."

He met her eyes, refusing to let her scare him.

"If you come after me, Christian, I will ruin you," she said. "Now, go grab your mop. The store's a disgrace."

CHAPTER 21

MERRY

By noon, Merry was broken.

Her shoes felt like they had pins in them from all the running around she had done, and her throat was sore from having to speak to customers all day. She'd said the same thing to almost everyone: "I'm so sorry, someone will be with you soon." Except the only "someone" on the floor was her, literally nobody else had shown up that morning and the entire jewellery department was in her hands.

After a couple of hours of being shouted at, Merry had slipped away and walked around in search of somebody to help her. It wasn't just her department that was understaffed, she saw, it was *every* department. Next door to her, in Lighting, one poor young guy called Ben was practically being swarmed by angry customers. It almost looked like something from a zombie movie, only with 'I Saw Mummy Kissing Santa Claus' pouring from the sound system.

Five minutes later, Merry returned to her till with the awful knowledge that she and Ben were literally the only two people on the entire floor. Customers milled around, growing increasingly frustrated, most of them leaving with tuts and moans. She did her best, but it was like fighting a rising tide, and eventually she resigned herself to the fact that she was destined to fail.

By one thirty, she was so desperate for the toilet that she literally ran from a customer as they were speaking. She flew through the staff door and into the nearest restroom, squeaking with relief as she sat down. She didn't hurry back, taking a moment to wash her hands and splash some water on her face. She gulped down a few sips, wondering if she'd even get a chance to have lunch today.

Think of the money, Merry, she told herself as she walked out of the restroom.

She was halfway down the corridor when she spotted somebody up ahead, standing alone by the staff door. They were holding something close to their face and when Merry got closer she saw that it was an envelope stuffed with some kind of paper.

"Diane?" she said.

Diane jumped, snapping the envelope closed and turning to Merry with a huge grin on her face. "Merry! Are you okay? You look like death."

"Yeah," said Merry. "It's been a tough shift. Speaking of which, any chance you can come help? The crowds out there are huge, and it's just me."

"No can do," said Diane. "I'm out of here."

"What do you mean?" Merry asked. "Are you working a half-day?"

Diane looked left and right down the corridor, then leaned in. "Have you not had an offer?" she whispered.

Merry shook her head. "No, what do you mean? What kind of offer?"

Diane held up the envelope. It was closed, but whatever was inside was making it bulge. "I shouldn't be telling you this, but somebody just gave me a huge pay check."

"What? Why?"

"To walk out the door," Diane said. "That's it. To just go."

"I don't understand," said Merry. "Who?"

Diane started to answer, but the staff door crunched open and Ben ran in.

"Can't stop! Must pee!" he yelled, racing for the men's restroom.

"You'll find out." Diane stuffed the envelope into her handbag. "But it's someone high up, someone from head office. Look, I've got to go. Hang around and you'll get yours too. Oh, and Merry?"

"Yeah?"

"I know I go on a lot about my rich boyfriend, and I'm not entirely sure I'd be with him if he was poor, but don't ever listen to a fool like me. It doesn't matter what somebody does for a living, not if you love them."

"Oh," Merry giggled. "I don't love . . . I mean, it's not like . . ."

"Whatever it is, you're not like that," said Diane. She winked at her, then walked through the door.

"It's *really* not like that," Merry said to herself as she walked back to her cash desk, but she wasn't entirely convinced herself. When was the last time a man had made her feel the way that Christian did? Even though things hadn't exactly been smooth between them, she still grinned every time he entered her head, like a kid waking up on Christmas Day. And he was as special as Christmas, she knew. You met somebody like that maybe once a *lifetime*, and when it happened you had to be ready to take a chance. You had to unwrap that present there and then, or you might never do it.

It was all so confusing, and it wasn't helped by the fact that as soon as she stepped out of the door she was attacked by a dozen people wanting her help. She fought through the afternoon as best as she was able, and by the time six o'clock rolled around she was on the verge of passing out. She tried to escape the next customer — a huge man in an expensive suit and bowler hat — but he actually grabbed hold of her arm to stop her from escaping.

"I demand service!" he roared. "Do you know how long I've been waiting?"

"I'm really sorry, sir," she said, trying to pull herself free. The man was so big that she was suddenly scared. "Please, I'm sure somebody else will—"

"No, not somebody else," he said. "You!"

There was a chime from overhead to signal an announcement.

"Would Merry Sinclair please come to the front desk," it said in a deep, melodious voice that sounded extremely familiar. "This is an emergency. Would Merry Sinclair please come to the front desk."

"That's me," she said to the man, pointing to her name tag with her free hand. "It's an emergency."

The man looked at her badge then let her go, huffing and puffing dramatically. Merry ran from him, rubbing her arm where he'd been holding her. She rode the staff elevator down, wondering what on earth could be happening that merited an emergency. Maybe they'd got a message from home, she thought as she ran across the atrium to the customer service desk. Maybe something had happened to her sister or . . .

Christian stood behind the desk, beaming at her. There was a queue of people in line waiting to be seen by one of the other members of staff there. He was wearing jeans and a dark blue sweater, and even though he still looked tired, his smile made Merry feel like she was waking up after a nine-hour nap.

"What's happened?" she said. "You called? There's an emergency?"

"Yeah." He walked out from the desk and, leaning in, kissed her on the cheek. "A very serious emergency."

She caught a whiff of something citrusy and fresh. He must have showered upstairs, she realised, and her mind flicked briefly to him standing naked under a torrent of hot water. She looked away, heat creeping up her neck.

"Is it my sister?" she snapped back to focus on the matter at hand.

Christian winced. "Shit, sorry," he whispered. "I didn't mean to panic you. It's nothing to do with anyone other than the two of us."

"Oh." Relief flooded though Merry's veins as she took his hand and he led her across the atrium, still smiling. It was contagious, because she started smiling too.

"What are you doing?" she said.

"Well, you said you weren't sure about coming to the ball with me tomorrow," he said. "And that's going to be a problem."

"Christian, what's going on?" she said. "What problem?"

"Well, I want to go to this famous ball seeing as I've heard so much about it. And I want to go with you." He shrugged. "If I can't go with you then I'm not going. And therein lies the problem."

"Honestly?" Merry stopped, tugging Christian to a standstill in front of her. "I can't afford to go because I have nothing to wear."

"Which makes you having nothing to wear now my problem too."

"I can't believe you used the public address system for that." Merry laughed. "You'll get in so much trouble!"

"It will be fine," he said. "They can't fire me, I'm the only janitor left. Well, apart from Harvey, who's about a hundred years old. To be honest, I walked past Jewellery on the way out and figured you needed some help escaping."

"I did," she said. "Thank you. I don't know what's going on right now, but it's getting bad. Where is everyone?"

For a moment, Christian's expression hardened. But then he smiled again. "Let's not worry about it. I've finished my shift, you've finished yours. Go grab your coat, and let's go fix this emergency."

CHAPTER 22

CHRISTIAN

"Where are we going?" Merry asked as they walked up Fifth Avenue, her arm locked in his. It was dark, but the Christmas lights that lined the streets made the city glow like a winter wonderland, and Merry herself seemed to glow with happiness as he led her along.

"You'll see," he replied. "I hope you don't mind."

"Mind what?"

Christian led her around the corner into the Rockefeller Plaza.

"More hot chocolate?" she asked.

Tempting, but he had an even better surprise. Christian steered her past the chocolate shop and stopped outside the sleek glass doors of the Devlin Storm flagship store.

Merry's steps faltered, just like he'd thought they would.

"Christian, what are we doing here?" She looked up at him with sad eyes. "I can't afford anything from this place. It's Devlin Storm — their window displays cost more than my rent."

"I knew you were going to say that."

"I don't think you can either, can you?" she went on. "I mean, Storm stuff is really expensive."

Christian took a deep breath. Once again, he wondered if he should just come clean and tell her everything. There was a good chance she'd hear him out, then forgive him, wasn't there? But they hadn't travelled far together, and it had been a rocky road in places. If he waited a few more days, until after the ball at least, then it would give him a chance to show her who he really was. That way, she wouldn't have to judge him on a single lie.

"What I'm about to tell you is going to sound crazy," he said. "But bear with me."

"Okay . . ." she said, one eyebrow rising.

"I actually know Devlin Storm. I happened to meet him once, while I was working overseas."

"Seriously?" Merry's mouth dropped open. "You know Devlin Storm?"

Christian nodded.

"And isn't he supposed to be, you know, a bit of a knob?" Merry asked. "That's what all the gossip says."

"He's an acquired taste," said Christian. "But not a bad guy when you get to know him. Anyway, I actually saved his life once."

"*Really*?" said Merry.

"Really," he said. "I helped him out in the mountains after he'd injured himself."

It was the truth, although he wasn't going to tell Merry everything that had happened. It had been a couple of years back, during a fundraiser in Colorado. The day after the actual event, they'd organised a cross-country trail, and he and Devlin had taken part. Devlin had been fitter, but he'd overstretched himself and while climbing a rocky slope in the middle of the mountains in the dead of night he'd slipped and fallen. Christian had carried Devlin back through a half-mile stretch of rocky wilderness to the club house, where he'd been treated for hypothermia and a snapped tendon in his knee.

"You saved Devlin Storm's life?" Merry shook her head. "That's just too weird not to be true."

"Anyway, he told me he owed me, big time," Christian said. "And that if I needed anything at all, I just had to call him. Well, call his *team*." He smiled at her. "So I did, this morning after we talked. I kind of guessed that not being able to afford an outfit was the main reason you didn't want to say yes to my invite. I hope I wasn't wildly off the mark?"

Her eyes darted away, embarrassed. "I didn't want to make a big thing of it."

"I know, that's why I didn't make a big thing of it either."

He had, after spending half the day wondering how he could buy Merry a new outfit for the ball without blowing his cover. He knew he could have taken her to any store in the city, and bought her absolutely any outfit she desired. But he would have had to tell her the truth, and more than that, he didn't think it would impress her. He had the funny feeling that if he threw money at her she would turn around and walk away. It was one of the things that drew him to her. Doing it this way was, ironically, much more honest.

"You literally tannoyed me through the whole of Carroll's." Merry laughed.

Christian grinned, pushed the door open and led Merry inside, where a smiling assistant swept over and offered Merry a glass of Prosecco.

"Go wild," he said. "Pick anything you like."

"Seriously?" Merry was breathless with excitement.

"Seriously. Merry Christmas!"

Merry squealed as the assistant led her away to the back of the store, and Christian laughed as he heard her gasping over the dresses and shoes.

He was still smiling when he heard the voice behind him.

"Well, well. If it isn't the janitor prince."

Christian turned to see Devlin Storm leaning against a marble pillar and eyeing him with his steely blues. He was wearing a sharply tailored black coat over an open-neck shirt

151

and slacks, his golden hair swept back like he'd just walked out of a photo shoot — which he probably had.

"Devlin, man." Christian pulled his friend in for a hug. "Didn't expect to you to be here tonight. It's so good to see you."

Devlin glanced past him towards the dressing rooms. "I wasn't going to stand by and let you shop here and not come say hi. Especially when there was a chance I could see Merry in the flesh. Plus, I promised the guys I'd report back."

"She doesn't know who I really am yet," Christian said. "Or how I really know you either, so maybe keep mum, yeah?"

Devlin arched a brow, amused. "Relax. I'm not about to blow your cover." He paused, folding his arms. "But how on earth does she think you're affording something from here?"

Christian shrugged, a grin playing at his lips. "I told her I saved your life."

Devlin blinked, then let out a bark of laughter. "You what?"

"I mean, I did. Technically."

"You dragged me half a mile through the snow because I was too stubborn to admit I'd torn something."

"You tried to jump a ravine and failed. That's on you."

Devlin shook his head, amused. "So, let me get this straight. You used our little misadventure as a cover story to explain how a janitor gets VIP access to my store?"

"Exactly."

Devlin clapped a hand on Christian's shoulder. "I'm impressed. That's some top-tier spin."

Christian smirked. "Well, you always said I'd missed my calling in PR."

"Just make sure she doesn't fall for the heroic part too hard, or she'll be devastated when she finds out the truth."

Christian's smile faltered for a split second. "Yeah. I know. I'm working on the timing."

Devlin studied him for a beat, then nodded once. "You really like her, don't you?"

Christian didn't answer. He didn't need to.

"Be careful. If you like her as much as I think you do, this is going to get a lot harder before it gets easier. If it ever gets easier."

Devlin gave Christian a look, then shifted his stance and glanced around at his own busy shop floor. "So, what's really going on with Carroll's? You any closer to finding out?"

Christian rubbed the back of his neck. "It's a mess. Half the staff are disappearing mid-shift and from what I've heard, they're being paid off."

"Paid off? That's bad. Any idea who's behind it?" Devlin frowned.

"Not yet. But it's someone with serious pull. Whatever's happening, it's coming from high up — too high for it to be some rogue worker."

Devlin went quiet for a moment, tapping a finger against his watch strap. Then he nodded. "Check the accounts."

Christian raised an eyebrow. "The accounts?"

"Payroll, discretionary budgets, supplier invoices — whatever you can get your hands on. Big payouts like that? They won't be marked 'mysterious bribe' or 'severance for no reason', but the money has to come from somewhere. It'll be hidden, but not invisible. You just have to know where to look."

Christian blinked, then gave a slow, impressed nod. "That's actually really good advice."

Devlin smirked. "I have my moments. Now go play Prince Charming before she comes back and catches us being all buddy-buddy."

Christian laughed under his breath, his tension easing for the first time in hours. "Thanks, Dev."

"Any time. Just don't wait too long to tell her who you are. If she's as special as you say, then girls like her don't come around twice."

CHAPTER 23

MERRY

It really was like Christmas!

There were no other customers on the VIP floor of the store, but three beautifully dressed sales clerks stood by and welcomed Merry off the elevator with smiles.

"We're all yours!" said one of the women, who was wearing a name badge that said Patricia. "Devlin says anything goes, anything you want."

"This is . . . I don't know what to say," Merry said, and it was true, she was speechless. "This is amazing."

"Our formal dresses are over here," said Patricia. "The winter range has been very popular this year."

She led Merry across the room to a display of elegant, mesmerisingly beautiful dresses of all shapes and colours. Two she recognised from red carpet interviews from TV, and one, she was sure, had been modelled by the First Lady during the last State of the Union address. None of them had a price tag, which wasn't surprising, but she knew from the limited range of Devlin Storm dresses they had at Carroll's that they retailed at thousands apiece. Sometimes tens of thousands.

"I really shouldn't." She bit her lip. "They're not really meant for somebody like me."

The soft chime of the elevator interrupted her and she turned to see Christian step out, his hands in his coat pockets, looking way more comfortable surrounded by thousands of dollars' worth of clothes than she felt.

"Merry." He grinned mischievously, his dark eyes shining. "Devlin owed me a favour and told me to pick whatever I wanted. But, let's be honest, none of these dresses are going to suit me, are they?"

He swept a hand towards the glittering rail and Merry giggled at the thought of Christian wrapped in a sequin number.

"And I'm still on my mission to give you the Christmas you deserve, so give yourself some credit and try on as many of these dresses as you like. Tell yourself you're doing it for me if it helps?"

He winked at her, a chorus of quiet "awwws!" rising up from the three sales clerks.

"What shall we try first?" Patricia asked.

Merry scanned the racks and hesitantly reached for a bright pink dress that shimmered under the lights. It was bold — louder than anything she'd ever worn — but something about it called to her.

She took it to the changing area, pulled the curtain closed and slipped into it. It fit like it had been stitched for her alone. The fabric hugged her in all the right places, the colour making her skin glow. And yet, as she turned in the mirror, her confidence wavered. Could she really pull this off? She felt like a walking highlighter pen. With a nervous breath, she stepped out of the fitting room.

Christian looked up and a smile popped on to his face. "Wow," he said, standing. "You're . . . wow."

"It's a bit much, isn't it?" she said, twisting a little. "I think I might be blinding the mannequins."

"You're lighting up the whole store," he said, eyes gleaming.

She laughed, but tugged at the neckline. "It's beautiful, but I don't think it's me."

"You sure?" he said. "Because you kind of look like the main character right now."

Merry bit her lip. "Could you help me out of it? The zipper's at the back and my arms aren't that bendy."

"Of course," he said, and followed her back into the fitting area without hesitation.

Inside the softly lit space, Merry turned her back to him. His hands were warm as they brushed her shoulder blades, carefully finding the zipper and sliding it down in one slow, smooth motion.

The dress slipped free pooling around her feet in a puddle of pink silk.

Before she could reach for the hanger, she felt Christian's lips press gently to the curve of her neck. A shiver ran through her as he kissed her again, slower this time, his hands settling lightly at her waist.

She closed her eyes, letting herself melt into the moment. But then her eyes drifted down to the dress, crumpled on the floor like it was nothing Thousands of pounds, just lying there like a discarded wrapper.

"Shoo," she whispered, picking up the dress and smoothing it out on the hanger. "Get outta here before someone sees you."

"Your wish is my command." Christian chuckled against her skin and disappeared back to his seat.

Merry lifted the hanger to a hook on the wall and caught sight of herself in the mirrors. Dressed just in her knickers, with work-weary hair, she had another jolt of guilt at taking up the store clerks' time when they could be tending to women who were meant to shop somewhere like this.

Patricia popped her head around the curtain with a genuine smile on her face and an armful of gorgeous dresses.

"Here you go," she said, hanging them up for Merry. "I thought these would work well with your colouring."

156

Merry's jaw actually dropped when she saw the dress that was still draped over Patricia's arm. It was perfect. There was literally no other word to describe it. She had never in her life seen a more perfect piece of clothing. It was black silk with hundreds of elegant, diamond-flecked snowflakes stitched into the shimmering fabric. It seemed almost like a living, breathing thing as Patricia held it up, the cloth unfurling to the floor.

"Oh!" said Merry.

"Nobody else in the world owns one of these," Patricia said, hanging that dress last. "Few people have even seen it. It's an exclusive — Devlin designed it for a leading lady whose name I can't tell you. She never wore it, because they fell out, and now here it is. She was about your size. Do you want to try it on?"

Merry nodded. *Oh, please be my size, please please please!*

Patricia helped her into it and by some magical fluke the dress flowed on to her like a second skin, cool and soft and impossibly comfortable. She hardly dared turn to face the mirror again, and when she did she barely recognised herself. The woman she saw stood tall and proud, her eyes bright and full of happiness, her smile beaming back from the glass.

"I . . ." Merry said. "I . . ."

It was too much. A tear escaped her eye, winding down her cheek.

"I'm sorry," she said.

"It's quite something," said Patricia.

Merry wiped the tears away, then turned to the curtain. Patricia pulled it to one side, and Christian's eyes widened as if he couldn't believe what he was seeing. He stood up slowly and walked to her.

"It looks like it was made for you," he said.

"It's amazing," Merry said.

He touched her arms gently, meeting her eyes. "You're amazing. This is all you. The dress is just the ribbon on the most perfect present I have ever seen."

157

"I can't take it," said Merry. "Can I? I mean, it must cost so much money. Shouldn't we check? I'm talking too much, I can't stop. It's just all so incredible. But I can't keep it. Can I?"

Christian laughed, opening his arms so that she could step into them. She rested her head against his chest, hearing that wonderful, reassuring thump of his heart, and he wrapped his arms around her.

"If she doesn't keep it, it'll be a tragedy," said a smooth voice from behind her.

Merry jumped slightly as Devlin Storm stepped out of the elevator, looking every inch the hot fashion-world aristocrat. He strolled towards them with the easy confidence of a man who owned the room — which, technically, he did. Merry felt like melting into the floor in a puddle of embarrassment at him seeing her in this incredible dress. Then she slowly realised what he had just said.

"Mr Storm, sir." She wasn't sure whether to curtsy or not, so she just bobbed a little on the spot.

"Devlin, please," he said with a grin, gesturing towards the dress. "And I've seen a lot of people in Storm gowns, but you here are a moment. If you don't take this one I will be personally offended. Don't forget to get the shoes and bag to match."

Then he turned to Christian and extended a hand. "Nice to see you again, sir."

Christian shook it, smiling and Devlin winked.

"Thanks for dragging me off that mountainside and, more importantly, for finding my dress its perfect owner. She wears it better than I ever imagined." He turned his attention back to Merry. "Man's a hero. Just don't let it go to his head. Must be off, places to be, people to piss off." And he vanished out of a side door in a waft of Chanel.

Merry stood frozen for a second. Then she squealed.

"Holy shit, I just met Devlin Storm!" she whisper-shouted, grabbing Christian's arms as if she might actually float away without something to hold on to. "He spoke to me! He called me the *perfect owner*! And he said I was a *moment*. Christian, I'm a moment!"

Christian chuckled. "You're more than a moment. You're an entire era."

Merry clutched her chest. "Okay, I need to take this off right now before I sweat through it and get banned from ever stepping foot in a Storm store again. This is not a dress you hyperventilate in. This is a dress you glide in gracefully. Without pit stains."

"I'll box it up for you," said Patricia, steering Merry back into the dressing room. Her head was buzzing as she undressed, and when she put her Carroll's dress back on it felt horribly tight and course. She wondered if this was what her life would feel like when Christian had gone, if it would turn back from something wonderful to something mundane and unbearable.

Just enjoy it, she told herself, and with a decisive nod she resolved to do exactly that. Slipping her shoes back on, she walked out of the booth for the final time to find Christian waiting there for her.

"You still look amazing," he said, and she laughed.

"Yeah, the Carroll's uniform really brings out the colour of my eyes." She ran a hand through her hair, watching Patricia box up the dress with a matching bag and a pair of shoes. "Are you really sure this is okay? I mean, I know you're not paying, but it was your favour. You could have used it for something important."

"I did," he said. "I used it for maybe the most important thing in my life. This was an emergency, remember? I want to go to that darn ball."

Patricia walked over with a bag, handing it to Merry.

Merry hesitated for a moment, then took it. "I can't thank you enough," she said. "I know you didn't have to show me this dress. I'm so happy you did."

"It's a perfect match," said Patricia. She looked at Christian, then at Merry, smiling.

Merry glanced at Christian, blown away again by how handsome he was even when he'd been standing next to a real-life rich person. Never _n a million years did she think she'd ever find herself on a date with a man like him, but then she never expected to be in a Devlin Storm shop holding a dress that had been designed for a movie star.

"Thank you, Christian," she said as the door closed behind them. She hugged the bag to her chest to shield it from the rain. "That was the nicest thing anyone has ever done for me. Again. You're good at making a girl feel special."

"It wasn't me," he said. "Thank Devlin. I'm just glad I could help. I can't wait to see you in it tomorrow."

"I hardly dare wear it," she said, and Christian laughed.

"Er, that was the whole point of this trip," he said. "Now you have to come to the ball with me. A taxi tonight, I insist. I've got to head back to work and you can't take the subway alone with a dress like that. You'd be asking for trouble."

"Can you afford it?" she asked, and he nodded.

"I did a few extra hours last night. It's fine."

"You're too good to me, Christian," she said. "I don't think I deserve it."

Christian stepped to the edge of the pavement and hailed a taxi. One pulled right over, and he opened the door, speaking to the driver. Merry saw him hand over some cash, and felt terrible that he had to part with even more money after such a generous gift. She'd pay him back for the taxi rides at least, she promised herself.

"Are you at work tomorrow?" he asked.

Merry nodded. "An early again, but it's not too bad because we close at three for the ball." She sighed. "I'm not sure I can face another day like today, though."

"Yeah, it was busy," Christian said. "So many people are leaving."

"Yeah, it's weird isn't it?" Merry said. "I saw Diane today, she's a girl I work with. She had an envelope, and I could have sworn it was full of cash."

Christian frowned, his eyes growing dark. "Cash?"

"Yeah, I don't know how much was there, but it was a lot. She told me she'd been given it in return for walking away, for literally walking out the door and never coming back."

"Did she say who gave it to her?" Christian asked.

Merry shook her head. "She wouldn't. But she told me it was somebody up high. It was somebody from head office."

Christian seemed to take the information in, nodding to himself.

"Get home safe, Merry," he said, holding the door for her. "I can't wait for tomorrow."

She paused for a moment, stepping up to kiss him good-bye. But there was something about Christian that had turned suddenly cold, his expression distant.

"Thanks again," she said as she climbed into the cab. "I really do mean it."

Christian nodded to her, then closed the door and walked away.

CHAPTER 24

CHRISTIAN

Somebody up high. Somebody from head office.

Merry's words rang in his head as he walked through the city. It was Margot. It had been her all along. And he had to tell his father.

Christian didn't have far to go. His family home, located on one of the most exclusive streets in the city, was only a short walk from Carroll's. He didn't take the fastest route along Fifth or Madison, though, preferring instead to walk through the park. He needed time to think, to work out what was going on, and to plan what he was going to say to his dad.

The facts were clear. Somebody was paying staff to leave Carroll's — a deliberate attempt to sink the store. That somebody worked in head office. His dad had always kept his management team small, to avoid complications in the line of command. There were only two people who worked out of head office. One was Lewis Carroll. The other was Margot.

And hadn't she pretty much admitted it to him when he'd confronted her?

Prove it, she'd said. What was that other than an admission of guilt? He could easily believe it, too. He knew how driven she was. They'd worked together on every aspect of company business, overseen by Lewis. But while Christian had been horrified by the conditions of the workers in the factories who supplied their goods, Margot couldn't have cared less. She'd wanted to increase their hours and cut their pay, and it had been an argument about this that had been the final straw for Christian. And now he knew she'd had a hand in him leaving too. It was all clicking into place.

Christian crossed in front of the Plaza Hotel, cutting between the carriages and the restless, blinkered horses — their great breaths appearing as clouds in the air — and walked into Central Park. It was busy, despite the hour and the weather, families and couples and tourists huddling against the cold as they laughed their way down the paths, between the rocks, through the trees. He'd loved it here so much when he was younger, especially at this time of year. It had been like his own personal back yard. After his mum had died, his dad had refused to even buy a Christmas tree, so Christian had come here to lose himself in the fairy lights and the snow. Of all the places in the world, the park felt most like home when it was Christmas.

He pulled up the collar of his cheap parka against the sleet. There were flecks of snow there, too, and he wondered if it would start to lie. Ahead, dozens of skaters whooped and cheered on the Wollman Rink, and he stopped for a moment to watch them. Merry skated into his mind, and suddenly, the stress of Margot just melted away. He thought of Merry's smile as she'd tried on the dresses in the Devlin Storm store, and he found himself smiling too. She stoked a fire inside him that was warm enough to thaw even the most frozen of hearts.

He wished she was here beside him right now, the heat of her body pressed against his, her head resting on his shoulder. All those years he'd walked through this park alone, and now he had somebody he might be able to walk through it with for ever. Could that really be possible? Could that Christmas dream really come true?

But he'd walked away from her just a few minutes ago because his mind had been on Margot, and on the store. If he and Merry had any chance of finding their happy-ever-after, then he had to solve this mystery and save Carroll's. And he had to make a decision about where his future lay.

The cold cut through his jacket like it was made of silk, and he shivered into motion again, passing the zoo. He cut back on to Fifth Avenue, crossing the street then walking swiftly up to East 69th. The street didn't give much away, but he knew the houses here were bigger than they looked, especially his father's. He stood in front of it, taking a deep, steadying breath. The mansion looked the same as it always had, and it felt weird being here after so many years away. But the truth was this house hadn't felt like home for a long, long time. It was just another place of business, an extension of his father, and of the store. And that thought made it all so much easier.

Walking up the short flight of steps to the gated entrance, he jabbed at the bell with a numb finger. Somewhere inside he heard a door slam, then the sound of footsteps. A few seconds later a muffled voice came from the speaker.

"The Carroll residence," it said in a British accent. "Who, may I ask, is calling?"

"Hey, Browick," said Christian, recognising the voice of the family butler. "It's me, Christian."

"Goodness," said the voice. "One moment."

The gate buzzed and Christian pulled it open, reaching the heavy double doors just as they opened. Browick was there, dressed in the same three-piece, black-tie suit he always wore, and looking older than the building itself. He smiled at Christian, nodding formally. "Master Christian," he said, his eyes glinting with happiness. "My dear boy. It has been too long."

"It has," said Christian. He grabbed the old man in a hug, breaking all the rules of etiquette that had been drummed into him as a kid. "How are you, old friend?"

"Old," he replied. "I should have retired years ago, but your father won't let me."

"Sure," said Christian, laughing. He knew for a fact that his dad had tried many times to offer the butler a substantial retirement package, so he could live out the rest of his years in peace and luxury, but Browick refused to leave. "Is he in? We need to talk."

"He's in the library," he said. "Can I take your coat? And make you tea?"

"That would be great," said Christian. "But can I have a scotch?"

Christian handed over the thin parka, laughing as Browick pulled an expression of distaste.

"Don't let his cold shoulder mislead you, Christian," Browick said. "He's missed you more than words can say."

Christian frowned, not sure what to make of what he'd just heard. The butler swept away without a sound, and Christian made his way through the empty lobby, running up the stairs. The mansion was vast, and it had always felt empty. Now it was more like a museum than anything else — too clean, too quiet and filled with old, unused things.

He stopped outside his mum and dad's room — or at least the room that they had shared before she had passed away. When she had gone, his father had moved all his things into one of the back bedrooms, and this room had become almost a shrine to his mother. It felt painful to be here again, after so long away, a pressure in his chest, in his heart, as he thought of all the times he had sought shelter with his mum in this room.

He heard his dad before he saw him — a run of deep, wheezing coughs echoing off the walls of the landing. Christian left the bedroom door closed and followed the sound into the duplex library, another wave of nostalgia sweeping over him as he remembered how much time he'd spent here as a child. It had always been his favourite room in the house, mainly because one of the few things his father had always done for him, even after his mother died, was read him stories. Back then, Lewis had seemed like a giant, even here among the thirty-foot-high shelves. But now he looked like a corpse, hunched over in an easy chair next to the roaring fire, and sucking oxygen through his mask.

"Dad?" Christian said, gently.

His father looked up, blinking for a moment as if he didn't recognise his own son. After a second or two, he smiled, but it seemed to take all his strength because his eyes drifted shut.

"Son." He said, pulling the mask away from his mouth. "You remembered how to find the place, then."

Christian ignored the comment, walking to the sofa that sat opposite his father's chair. Despite the chill of the atmosphere, the huge room felt wonderfully cosy, and the pop and snap of the logs in the fire made Christian shiver with delight. He studied the books, spotting the spines of the ones he'd loved to read as a boy. The sight of them made him feel impossibly sad, and he spoke his next words through a lump in his throat.

"You know why I left, Dad."

Lewis waved the words away, opening his watery eyes and staring at Christian. "You made your choice."

"I did, but it wasn't just mine," said Christian. "I was only ever a tool to you, somebody to carry on your legacy. I needed to break away from this empire of yours. I had no idea if it would be for ever, but then you took the choice away from me when you banished me."

"Rightfully so," his dad muttered. "You were so ungrateful. After everything I did for you, everything I gave you."

Even though he'd promised himself he wouldn't get angry, Christian felt the familiar, awful rage rising inside him.

"Everything you gave me?" he said, meeting his dad's eyes.

"You had everything money could buy," his dad growled.

"All I wanted was you, Dad." Christian took a deep breath, forcing himself to calm down. "Ever since Mum died, it was like . . . it was like *you* died too. Right when I needed you. You just weren't there anymore."

166

Lewis scoffed, but his expression was one of hurt. He sucked a breath through his mask, and Christian waited for the angry response, for the argument. But his dad just hung his head.

"I know," he said, his admission of guilt shocking Christian so much he didn't know what to say. "It was too hard, Christian, after she'd gone. You're right. A piece of me went with her and I never got it back. Help me up, son."

Christian did as he was asked, helping his father stand. The old man wheezed and limped his way to the bookcase beside the fire. After a moment of searching, he pulled a novel from the shelf. It was a first edition of *The Lion, The Witch, and the Wardrobe*, and seeing it again after all these years brought back so many memories that Christian felt dizzy with the force of them.

"You remember it," said his dad.

"Of course." Christian took the book and blew the dust from it. "Mum gave it to me. She wrapped it up and hid it among the fake presents beneath the tree in the store. It's so weird, I was just thinking about this. I can't believe you've still got it."

"Of course I do," his dad said. "I know I wasn't a good father to you, Christian, certainly not after Olivia died, and probably not much before that, either. You probably remember Christmases when I wasn't there."

Christian nodded. They had been exactly that. Most years his dad hadn't been there to give him his presents, Browick had done it instead.

"But you have to understand how hard it was," his dad went on, staring at the flames. "It was your mother's favourite time of year, and the only good I saw in it died with her. I just couldn't bring myself to be happy without her, not even for you. And for that, I'm sorry. But you're wrong about something."

"What?" Christian asked.

"That book. Your mum didn't buy it for you. I did."

"No," said Christian. "I remember it — she wrapped it for me and left it there after you told me off for opening the display presents."

Lewis smiled sadly. "I did tell you off," he said. "And I felt rotten for it. So I bought you the book to say sorry. I wrapped it and hid it beneath the tree, and I was going to be there when you opened it, only something came up. I can't remember what — store business. It was always store business." He sighed. "So your mum did it."

He paused, then reached into his pocket. "Same year I gave this to your mum. Here, you keep it now."

He pulled out a small velvet box and handed it to Christian. Inside was a delicate spiral necklace that made Christian's heart ache as he vividly remembered his mum wearing it. Christian stared at it for a long time, the past catching up to him in a quiet rush. Lewis looked up at him, and Christian noticed that for the first time in his life he was taller than his father.

"You might not remember, son, but we did have good times, lots of them, even after she died. Every Christmas Eve we sat right here and opened new books, reading them by the fire. I wish I'd been there for you more. There's not a day that goes by I don't wish I'd done things differently, or that we had the chance to do it again. But hey, we don't get to turn back time. We only get to look forward, right?"

"Right," said Christian. He hadn't expected this at all, and the sudden rush of emotion paralysed him.

His dad wheezed in a breath, coughing loudly. Then he took Christian's hand in his, his skin as cold as marble. For a moment, Christian wondered if his father would tell him more about the good times. But it was just store business. It was *always* store business.

"You're here. You have something to tell me?"

"I do," said Christian, sighing. He held his father for a moment, then let go. "I found something out."

His dad's expression sharpened. "Yeah?"

"Yeah," said Christian, taking a deep breath. "Somebody is paying people to leave Carroll's. Somebody is deliberately sabotaging the store."

His dad's breaths came in great, gulping wheezes as he took in what he was being told.

"Somebody is giving cash payouts to anyone who leaves," Christian went on. "Somebody wants this business to die. At first, I thought it might be another store, somebody trying to put Carroll's under before Christmas. But then I did some digging. Dad, I know who's doing this."

"I know what you're thinking," said Lewis. "It's not Margot."

"Are you sure?" Christian asked. "She's got a lot to gain."

"And a lot to lose," his dad said. "Margot's been good to me. If she was my own family, then she would be in charge, I have no doubt about it. It's not too late, you know."

"Too late for what?" Christian asked, frowning.

"For you to change your mind and come back permanently. Find someone to marry, settle down and have kids to pass on the family name."

"Dad, whoa," said Christian, holding up a hand. "This isn't medieval England — you can't just marry your children off to continue your legacy. I'm here to help you save Carroll's, that's all. But if you won't even listen to what I'm telling you I've found, then I don't know what to do. If Margot thinks she can get what she wants by bringing the store to its knees, then marching in to save it, that's exactly what she'll do. Either that or somebody else has promised her the top job in another company if she can force us into bankruptcy."

"It's not that bad," said his dad.

"It is," said Christian. "We're just days away from Christmas and the store is sinking fast. There's nobody out there anymore. People are leaving without buying, going elsewhere."

"So, *you* save it," said his dad, looking right at him. "Quit your job overseas, come back to us full-time — not as a janitor, but as the CEO."

"I . . ."

Christian hesitated, a thought needling itself into the back of his brain. This encounter had been so unexpected. His dad had always been one to launch straight into an argument, to avoid any kind of emotional exchange. But he was being so open, so honest.

It's because he's dying, Christian thought, chasing the unbearable words away with a shake of his head. But it was true. Nothing made you more honest than death. Nothing made you more open to reconciliation.

Nothing made you more desperate.

"Oh God, Dad. It's not Margot, is it?" Christian said, the realisation like a flashbang going off inside his skull. "Oh, Dad, no. It's *you*. You're paying people off. You're bringing down the store."

His dad didn't look at him. He just stared at the fire, his sad eyes full of reflected flames.

"But why, Dad? It doesn't make any sense."

Only it *did* make sense. It made an awful kind of sense.

"It was the only way," Lewis said after a moment.

"The only way to bring me back," said Christian. "But you could have just asked. You could have just opened up to me."

"I did ask," said his father. "I asked a hundred times. I just didn't ask the way I should have. Then it was too late. I knew that you wouldn't come back for me, but that you might come back for the store. Let's face it, in some ways it was more of a parent to you than I ever was. It sheltered you, it cared for you, it was always there for you."

Lewis sighed, then turned to Christian. A tear wound its way over the wrinkles of his face and Christian watched it, aghast. He couldn't ever remember seeing his father cry before.

"I'm not trying to kill the store. I was never going to let it get that bad, at least I tried not to," he said. "I just wanted you back in my life. I don't know how long I've got, and I just wanted the chance to see you again, to make it all okay. And you're here, which means so much to me. You're here, and you care — about me, about the store, about everything."

"Of course I do, Dad," Christian said. "Always. I love you."

"I love you too, son," his dad said, opening his arms. Christian held his father, feeling how weak he was, hearing the rattle of his lungs as he breathed. He was shocked, and there was a trace of anger there at what he'd just discovered, but it was drowned by the force of the love he still held for the old man. His head was full of memories flowing into his mind like a dam had burst — memories of trips to the park, to the zoo, out on the boat on the river. Memories of his mum and dad lifting him up between them in the autumn, the falling leaves like flames. And memories of Christmas, those early years when he'd woken up in the morning and found his father cooking breakfast in the kitchen, a mountain of presents beneath the tree.

His dad was right — there had been good times. But Christian had been so focused on the bad that he'd forgotten them.

"I want you to take a long, hard look at yourself, Christian," Lewis said, coughing into his oxygen mask. "I want you to ask yourself what you're really running away from. And I want you to think — really think — about whether there is something here, in this family, in this city, in this store, that is worth staying for."

Christian started to reply, but something kept the words from coming out. He took a deep breath, thinking about his family — how only his dad remained. He thought about the city, a city that had once offered him so much hope, and he thought about the store. What *was* he running from?

"I want you to be happy, and to be happy here." His dad went on. "It's not much to ask, is it? Let's make this a new start. This is the last chapter of my life, son, so let's read this one together, please?"

Christian looked down at the fire, feeling the warmth of it against his skin, losing himself in the flickering flames. If he could just make it work with Merry, then being happy and being here, in New York, wasn't much to ask at all. He was tired of travelling.

He took a deep breath, making a decision right there.

"I'll stay."

For his dad, for the store, and for Merry.

CHAPTER 25

MERRY

Merry packed everything she needed for the ball carefully in her holdall and skipped across town, arriving at work five minutes early — which had to be a record for her. She hung the dress in her locker, giving the handbag a quick kiss before changing into her uniform. She hadn't heard from Christian at all since they'd parted, but then they hadn't even exchanged numbers yet. Or surnames.

Which was weird, given what they had already exchanged.

It made her pause for a moment, one shoe half on, as the reality struck her. They'd flown into each other's lives like a toboggan run and part of her was worried they'd moved *too* quickly, that they should slow things down a bit.

But part of her just wanted to ride with it. This had been her Christmas wish, after all, and it seemed that Santa had granted it, bells and whistles included.

The schedule told her that she was on greeter duty today, which she wasn't too sad about. Another day on Jewellery might have been the end of her. Putting on her itchy Santa hat, she made her way downstairs and offered a beaming smile to the first few customers of the day. There must have been something honest about it because it was contagious. People looked at her and smiled back, their happiness providing a warmth that easily countered the cold.

Just after eleven, she heard a familiar rumble of wheels and she turned to see Christian behind her. It was all she could do not to pounce into his arms.

"Hi!" Her cheeks erupted into a monster blush for absolutely no reason.

"Hey," he said. "How are you?"

"Good," she said. "Great! I'm so excited about the dance."

"Me too," he said. "I . . ." He stopped speaking, shaking his head as if he couldn't believe what he was about to say. "I missed you last night, after you'd left."

A delighted laugh escaped Merry's mouth before she could stop it, and she clapped a hand over her lips before the customers noticed.

"Really?" she said.

"Really." He smiled at her, his deep, brown eyes big enough to lose herself in for days. "Sorry, that's a really weird thing to say."

"It's not," she said. "I mean, I missed you too. My bed was freezing!"

Christian laughed, and he looked like he was going to say something else when somebody cleared their throat behind Merry. She spun around to see Mrs Cradley there, the Dragon Lady tapping her foot impatiently. But there was a twinkle in her eye — even she couldn't be entirely miserable on the day of the dance.

"I'm going!" Christian said, running off with his trolley. "I know, I know, those soap dispensers won't fill themselves!"

Merry laughed, directing the next customer to the restaurant as Mrs Cradley stalked away. The store was busier than ever, which at least made the time fly by. At 2.50 p.m. the Christmas music stopped and an announcement went out to say that the store was closing early. Half an hour later, the last few recalcitrant customers were herded out of the building. Merry took off her hat and scratched her head, only to hear what sounded like an excited dolphin racing towards her.

"Squeeeee!"

She spun around in time to see Alice flying across the lobby. Her friend jumped up and down in delight.

"The ball! The ball!"

Merry laughed, taking Alice's outstretched hands and letting her spin them both around.

"Aren't you excited, Merry?" Alice asked. "It's going to be so much fun. I can taste the champagne already!"

"That's because she's already cracked open a case or two," said Trudy, walking up.

"I have not," said Alice. "But I did sneak a canapé earlier when the caterers came in. They're delicious. Are you going to get changed?"

"It's a little early, isn't it?" said Merry. "It doesn't start until seven, right?"

"That doesn't stop three glamorous ladies from hitting the bar first," said Trudy. "Anyone up for it?"

There was only one person in the entire city that Merry wanted to see right now, but she knew that Christian would be on duty getting the store ready for the ball. She didn't really fancy drinks, but four hours was a long time to hang around by herself.

"Sure," she said. "I'm game."

They rode to the top floor in the customer elevators, and Merry grabbed her bag and her jacket, leaving everything else in her locker. She had to resist the temptation to pull the dress out and caress it.

They made their way down Fifth Avenue to the same place where she and Christian had shared their hot chocolate. It felt like something that had happened years ago, Merry thought as they stepped out of the worsening weather into the warmth of the bar. It felt like the kind of memory she should be sharing with her children, or even her grandchildren. It was such a strange sensation — that she'd somehow lived a whole lifetime in these short few days. Nothing that had happened before that night felt real anymore.

"Earth to Merry," said Trudy, shaking her out of her daydream.

"She's got it bad," said Alice, smiling.

"Oh yeah," said Trudy. "She's got it *seriously* bad."

"I don't!" squeaked Merry. "I'm just . . . tired."

"Tired of being alone," said Trudy with a laugh.

"Tired of not having a man to kiss," added Alice, wrapping her arms around herself and smooching the air. Merry slapped her gently on the shoulder and they took a seat by the window, all of them giggling. Christmas songs were playing, and outside, the sleet was slowing into snow — huge, fat flakes drifting down from the darkening sky. The lights were buzzing to life, breathing Christmas spirit into every building. The waitress — Diane's cousin — took their orders, winking at Merry, and Merry found herself grinning so hard her cheeks hurt.

They ordered champagne to start. Even though Trudy and Alice chatted freely about work, and their lives outside the store, Merry found it difficult to keep up. The entirety of her mind was taken up by Christian — his smile, his warm eyes, his infectious laugh, his strong arms, not to mention those hands . . . Every time she found herself thinking of him she had to catch herself before her cheeks exploded.

". . . reminds me," Alice was saying when Merry tuned into the conversation again. "There might not even be a job to go back to next year."

"What do you mean?" Trudy asked.

"The store, haven't you heard?" Alice leaned in and they all crowded around her. "It's going under. Poor Lewis Carroll is ill. I heard he's dying. The store won't go on without him."

"It has to," said Merry. "I need this job."

"At least we won't have to answer to Cradley anymore," laughed Alice.

"That's true," said Merry.

"Anyway, I heard that Carroll's son is back in town," said Trudy. "That he's going to take over."

"I didn't know he had a son," said Merry.

Trudy nodded, taking a sip of her drink. "Yeah, he used to work here, apparently, in the head office. He left, some disagreement or other. But anyway, I heard he's back, and I heard he's gorgeous."

"Rich and gorgeous," said Alice, purring. "I wonder if he'll be there tonight?"

"I can think of a certain somebody who needs a rich boyfriend," said Trudy, looking at Merry.

Merry squirmed uncomfortably, remembering the conversation that Christian had overheard a couple of days ago. "I don't care how rich he is," she said. "You can't fall in love with notes and coins."

"That's true enough." Alice checked her phone. "Anyway, it's nearly five. It's time to go and get ready."

The snow had doubled in strength and they ran through it back to Carroll's, bursting into the store like kids at Christmas. The absence of customers made the space look so much bigger, and the enormous Christmas tree rose majestically through the open levels. Everywhere Merry looked there were lights and ribbons, holly and mistletoe, baubles and tinsel. It made her heart feel light with happiness to see such festive joy.

They made their way up to the locker room together. Even though so many people had left the store recently, the place was still busy as people changed out of their uniforms and into their formal dresses. Merry marvelled at the beautiful fabrics and striking colours, the sparkle of silver and the glint of gold. Everybody was chatting and laughing, the atmosphere positively electric, but when Merry opened her locker door and pulled out her dress the room fell eerily quiet.

"Oh my God," said Trudy. "That's a Storm dress."

Merry turned around, holding the dress protectively against her chest. It clung to her, as though it wanted to be worn, the tiny, bejewelled snowflakes flashing like diamonds.

Trudy walked up, her eyes wide with sheer astonishment. "I saw that dress in *Vogue*," she said. "It was supposed to be for that actress, the Oscar winner. You know the one. It was custom designed by Devlin Storm himself, but then they fell out and she never wore it. How . . . how on earth have you got it?"

Merry almost felt embarrassed, and she wondered if maybe it was too much, if maybe the sight of an ordinary girl like her in such a glorious and expensive dress would make people laugh — or make them angry. But she refused to let anything stop her from enjoying this moment. This was Christian's gift to her, and that's all that mattered.

"It was a present," she said. "A very generous one."

"It can't have been a gift from your cleaner boyfriend," Trudy said. "So who?"

Alice smiled kindly. "It doesn't matter who. You're very lucky. It's beautiful. Go on, put it on!"

Merry grinned, stripping out of her uniform and slipping into the dress. She turned around and Alice zipped it up.

"Oh, wow," Trudy said with a hint of envy. "That's . . . that's just something else."

"Oh, Merry, you look incredible!" shouted Alice, hugging her. She grabbed Merry's shoes from the locker. "Sit there, let me do your hair."

Merry did as she was told, feeling like royalty as Alice started brushing her hair. Even though Trudy rolled her eyes, she joined in, expertly twisting Merry's stubborn red locks into elegant braids. Merry sat there like a blushing bride as the two girls did her makeup, trying not to laugh as they tickled her cheeks with brushes and her lips with gloss. She had no idea how long they worked on her, but after a while they stood back in awe.

"Whoa, mamma," said Trudy.

Alice grinned. "You look like a movie star."

Merry looked into the mirror, studying her reflection the way that somebody might watch a movie. And the person she saw there *belonged* in a movie, a movie where a girl made a Christmas wish to become a princess, where she fell in love with her prince and waltzed with him into the sunset. Merry grinned at herself, wondering if this was too good to be real life, if maybe this movie was about to end. But what if it didn't?

"Thank you," she said, almost too emotional to get the words out. "I don't know what to say. Everyone has been so kind to me."

"Sometimes the world *is* kind." Alice tucked a wisp of hair behind Merry's ear. "A lot of the time it's cruel, but these moments are the ones we live for. You do look beautiful, Merry. Go and enjoy this moment of kindness. Go live your fairy tale."

Merry stood up, the dress flowing perfectly, the shoes fitting like a dream.

Please let this be an amazing evening, she thought. *Please let Alice be right, let this be my fairy-tale happy-ever-after.*

But in the back of her mind she thought of last Christmas Day, sitting alone at her kitchen table crying into a cold turkey, and she hoped that this story, like all the fairy tales she could remember, didn't have a nasty twist.

CHAPTER 26

CHRISTIAN

Christian walked out on to the ballroom floor, fastening his cufflinks as he went.

It wasn't really a ballroom, of course. It was the eighth floor of Carroll's, more commonly known as the restaurant. It was a vast, open space, and it looked even larger now that the tables and chairs had been cleared out. After his shift had finished that afternoon, he and Harvey had given the space a deep clean, and then a team of event managers had moved in to arrange the décor. Now it looked like something from a homecoming prom, with every wall covered in glittery tinsel and literally hundreds of lights and baubles hanging from the ceiling.

The most impressive thing, though, was the view through the huge windows. The skies were dark now, but finally the snow had arrived and it was falling fast and hard. It was settling, too, making Fifth Avenue glow in the lights that adorned every building. A twenty-four-piece swing band had set up in front of the windows, led by an amazing female singer, and they were currently belting out a range of Christmas songs.

They were so good that Christian expected to see Bing Crosby stroll out at any moment, a microphone in his hand and that famous smile on his face.

He straightened the lapels of his suit, one he hadn't worn in years. It felt a little tight against the muscles he'd developed overseas, but it was comfortable enough. His head was ringing from his visit home. He'd spent all night thinking about his father's words and feeling bad about them too. All these years he'd blamed him for ruining Christmas, for making life miserable, but not once had he thought about how his dad must have felt. It must have been so hard carrying on as normal after Mum died. He'd done his best, Christian remembered that now. It hadn't always been enough, but it had been something.

He still couldn't believe his father was responsible for sabotaging his own store, but he understood why he'd done it. It had been the only way to bring Christian home. And now it would stop. Now, at least, Carroll's would start to recover. Christian would make sure of it.

"Drink, sir?" asked a waitress, offering him a glass of champagne from a silver tray.

"No, thank you," he said.

She looked him up and down, fanning her face with her free hand as she walked away. The band had switched to a lively jazz version of 'Jingle Bells', the singer belting out the words with such gusto that even Christian found himself tapping his feet. The crowd were going wild, people whooping as they danced.

There had always been a ball at Carroll's. They'd been a New York tradition for over a hundred years. Christian's granddad, Cornelius, had started them way back in the roaring twenties, and Lewis had taken them on. Christian vividly remembered them from his childhood, dancing with the staff, having his hair ruffled by the perfume girls, and always joining in with the band, singing seasonal numbers on the microphone in his squeaky voice. Even the year that his mum died, his dad had made sure the ball went ahead, although that year most of the staff had worn black to honour her.

This year there was a festival of colour in the room — two hundred people or more in sensational dresses and well-fitting suits. Christian recognised a few from his time in the store, but he knew that there would be plenty of people here who'd won a ticket on the famous Carroll's lottery. Some were dancing, others already attacking the buffet that stretched the entire length of the room.

There was only one person he was interested in seeing, though. He searched the crowds, looking for Merry. He was giddy with excitement at the thought of seeing her, and that wasn't just a turn of phrase — he actually felt light-headed. He couldn't remember ever feeling this much anticipation before a date, not even back in high school. It had just gone seven, and he knew she'd be here soon, but the anticipation of seeing her fizzed like electricity inside his head.

Then he turned, and there she was.

Holy fuck. His heart paused for a moment as he took in what he saw. She swept into the room in a swirl of black and silver. The dress looked stunning on her, but it was *her* that he saw — her amazing smile, her eyes bright with excitement.

Merry moved first, weaving through the crowd. Christian met her halfway, pulling her into a fierce, breathless hug. He almost fumbled the gift in his hand, but didn't care. She held on to him tightly, her laughter warm against his neck and, for a moment, everything else disappeared.

Christian didn't want to let go. Not now. Maybe not ever. He buried his face in her shoulder, breathing her in — warm skin, a trace of perfume, something inherently compelling. His hands slid down her back, and rested on the rise of her hips.

"I've been going out of my mind," he murmured against her ear. "You look — God, Merry, you look . . ."

She pulled back just enough to meet his eyes. "So do you."

Christian didn't hesitate. He dipped his head and kissed her, slowly at first, but the second her mouth parted for him,

181

something in him ignited. The world blurred. Her lips were soft and warm, her body pressed flush against his, and he felt a sudden pulse of desire that made his grip on her hips tighten.

Merry made a soft sound and he deepened the kiss instinctively, for a second forgetting they were in public.

When he finally pulled back, she was breathless, her cheeks flushed, lips kiss-bruised and curved in a smile that did dangerous things to him.

"Wow," she said softly, eyes dark with something that matched the heat in his own.

"Yeah," he said. "Sorry, that got intense."

"And here I was worried you might go in for a polite cheek kiss," she teased.

"Not a chance," he said, voice still rough. "I've been thinking about doing that since I last saw you. Here, I have something for you."

"You've already given me too much," she said as he reluctantly let go of her. "I can't accept anything else."

"This is different." He held out the box, beautifully wrapped in shiny, red paper. "Please. Open it."

With shaking fingers, Merry picked at the paper, carefully opening the present. Inside was a black box, and when she opened it her jaw dropped.

"Do you—" Christian started, worried that she hated it. "I mean, if you don't . . "

"I love it." She gently took the elegant silver chain out of the box and held it up in front of her. Hanging from the end of it was the beautiful silver spiral that had once belonged to his mum, that now spun magically in the air in front of her. "Oh, Christian, I love it so much. But you shouldn't have."

"I didn't buy it," he said. "It belonged to my mum."

Merry looked past the spiral, and he could barely see her face through his sudden blur of tears. He cleared his throat.

"She loved spirals," he said. "They always reminded her of life, of love. Things don't always seem to be going in the direction you want them to, but—"

"You're always moving forward," Merry said alongside him.

He smiled at her, frowning. "How did you know?"

"Because she's right."

"May I?" he said, and she turned, allowing him to fasten the necklace. The glittering spiral complemented the dress completely, a perfect finishing touch. He took Merry in his arms again, leaning down and kissing the top of her head.

And in that moment, something shifted in him. It was like the loose strands of his life — the lies, the half-truths, the guarded pieces he'd held back — began to weave themselves into something whole again. He felt it settle in his chest with quiet certainty. After tonight, he was going to tell her everything.

"Let's dance." He held out his hand and Merry took it.

The band had switched songs, and one of the clerks from the store had taken the mic, belting out a Nat King Cole tune with a pretty good voice. Christian and Merry danced together, not a care in the world. They danced as if they knew the night would go on for ever.

It was only when the crowd started to clap that Christian looked up. The song had finished and the girl with the microphone left the stage with a curtsy.

"Any other takers?" said the singer from the band, offering the microphone to the audience.

"How about it?" asked Christian. "A duet?"

Merry laughed, then realised he was being serious. "In front of all these people? No way!"

"It doesn't have to be for them," he said. "It's just for us."

Merry hesitated. "Okay," she said, laughing. "Okay, let's do it."

He took her hand, leading her through the crowd. People started cheering as they saw them, and the singer handed the microphone to Christian.

"Any requests?" the singer asked.

Merry smiled. "'Baby It's Cold Outside?'" she replied, looking at Christian.

He nodded enthusiastically. "You read my mind."

The band kicked off, the music almost overpowering. It was incredible, intoxicating, especially when Christian lifted the microphone to his mouth. For a moment, his mind a drew a blank. Then the words began to flow.

The rest of the room seemed to melt away until it was just the two of them. Merry held Christian's hand, singing her heart out just for him. It really was as if they had been put under a spell, a wonderful, unbreakable spell that would hold them in this moment like a snow globe.

They sang the last line together, reaching a crescendo.

The band ended the song with a flourish, and the crowd broke into rapturous applause, the sound of it pulling Merry back to the real world. She looked around, feeling suddenly sheepish at standing there in front of everyone. But there was so much goodwill in the room, so much warmth, that she quickly found herself smiling again.

Christian handed the microphone back to the singer and hugged her, both of them laughing into each other.

"That was amazing," he said, and she nodded, about to reply, when Christian saw something from the corner of his eye that made his blood run cold.

His dad was in the room and he was heading in their direction.

CHAPTER 27

MERRY

The applause was thunderous, but Merry barely heard it. Her pulse was still racing, her skin buzzing from the adrenaline of performing and the even more surreal feeling of singing a duet — a Christmas duet, no less — with Christian. The moment felt so impossibly perfect that she wanted to bottle it, store it somewhere safe so she could revisit it forever.

He looked devastatingly handsome, his eyes crinkled with laughter, his jawline dusted with stubble, and his smile was still doing dangerous things to her equilibrium. He hugged her close and she breathed in the scent of him. How had this happened? How had she, Merry Sinclair, the girl who was always late, always chaotic, and never sparkly, ended up here? In a twinkling ballroom, draped in silk, arms around a man who looked at her like she was made of magic. She tilted her head up to ask him how she'd got so lucky when she saw his expression shift.

Merry followed his gaze, still breathless and slightly dazed, and spotted the source: a man walking steadily through the crowd, silver-haired and upright, but a lot less commanding than the last time she'd seen him. Mr Lewis Carroll.

Merry stepped gently out of Christian's arms, grabbed his hand and the pair of them slipped off the stage as Lewis approached the microphone. The crowd noticed, too, the murmur of conversation slowly draining away as the room quieted. Lewis reached the mic, the bright stage lights catching the hollows beneath his eyes.

"Thank you," he said, and though his voice was gravelly with age, it rang clear. "Thank you all for being here."

Merry and Christian slipped into the crowd, her heart still fluttering as she tucked herself behind a pair of perfume girls who were whispering to each other about the possibility of a younger Carroll being in the room.

"If I could just have a few moments of your time," Lewis continued, his hand resting gently on the mic stand, "I'd like to say a few words."

The room was silent now. Even the clinks of the bottles and glasses at the bar had stopped. Snow continued to fall outside the vast windows behind him, the lights of Fifth Avenue glowing through the blur.

"As many of you know, Carroll's has had . . . a difficult season. And the truth is, a great deal of that is on me."

Merry felt a ripple move through the room.

Lewis adjusted his cuff and looked out at the crowd. "I haven't been well. And I've made decisions that didn't always make sense to anyone but me. I owe you all an apology — for the stress and uncertainty and the cuts."

Merry felt her throat catch. She glanced at Christian by her side. He was standing tall, but he was also visibly tense.

Lewis continued. "But tonight isn't about me. Tonight is about something better. It's about the future of Carroll's and the hope that I have for it to blossom in younger hands. I am stepping down as Chairman of Carroll's Department Store. Effective immediately."

Gasps rang out across the ballroom.

"And I'm thrilled to tell you that my son will be taking over. He's here tonight to meet you all. Now, if only I was wearing my glasses, I'd be able to see him."

The room erupted in fresh applause and people started glancing around the space to see if they could catch a glimpse of the young man. Merry felt excitement bubble in her at the idea that her job was safe and things might start getting a bit easier on the shop floor. She nudged Christian to give him a thumbs up, but he looked like he wanted to set fire to the building.

"Christian?" She leaned into him with her shoulder. "What's up?"

Lewis raised his hand again, commanding the room. "Please, everyone, give a warm welcome to the new leader of Carroll's — my son, Christian Carroll!"

Merry's stomach dropped. No. No, it had to be a coincidence. But then Christian faltered beside her, his jaw tensed, his hands fisted at his side. Then, without a word, he stepped forward and climbed the stairs to the stage.

Merry watched him go, her breath trapped in her chest.

She hadn't imagined it. It was him. Christian Carroll. *The* Christian Carroll, son and heir of the Carroll empire.

She thought back to all the moments they'd shared together, each one now prickling with betrayal. That first conversation at the café, when he'd acted like he'd randomly bumped into her. The date he'd planned so carefully, with its perfect timing and thoughtful details. The stories he'd told her. The way he'd touched her, held her, kissed her like she was the only thing on his Christmas list.

And the sex. God, the sex. She'd given herself to him completely, heart wide open, soul bare. She'd let him in and trusted him. She'd believed every word he said. All while he was living a lie. He'd *known*, and he'd let her keep believing.

Why hadn't she seen it sooner? The ease with which he moved through the store. The way he talked about leadership and legacy. The tiny, careful things he'd avoided saying. Of course he had been hiding something.

She'd been so naive. So wrapped up in her own fantasy that she hadn't questioned the magic. She'd wanted her Christmas wish to come true so badly that she hadn't stopped to think about the cost. And now here she was, standing in a glitter-drenched ballroom, surrounded by strangers, feeling like the biggest fool in New York.

She tried to swallow the lump in her throat, but it wouldn't budge, while around her, her friends were squealing with excitement. On stage, Christian took the microphone from his father.

"Thank you," he said, commanding attention. "I know this might come as a surprise to some of you, but for the past few weeks, I've been working undercover on the shop floor. Getting to know the store from the inside out. Learning from all of you because I've been away for such a long time."

A murmur spread through the room and Merry stopped breathing.

"It was important to me," Christian continued, "to see Carroll's through fresh eyes. To understand the challenges you face, the systems that are broken, the pressures you're under. I didn't want to come in as just another Carroll. I wanted to earn the right to lead."

More laughter and applause, but Merry's ears were ringing. So that was it. She hadn't just been left out of the truth. She'd been part of his strategy. He'd embedded himself in the store like a secret shopper, gathering intel. She remembered the way he had quizzed her about staffing numbers — he'd even asked her if she knew what was making Carroll's feel weird lately.

Oh my God, I'm such an idiot.

Tears stung her eyes.

"There you are!" Someone grabbed her arm — a wide-eyed Trudy. "You knew, didn't you? That's why you were so grossed out by the idea of dating a janitor."

"What the hell, Merry?" another voice chimed in. Ben this time, his eyebrows raised. "Were you, like, in on it? Were you spying on me?"

"I can't believe you kept that a secret," said Alice, stepping in close, hurt etched on her face. "Come on, Merry, spill. Did you know who he was this whole time?"

"Merry," Trudy said, serious now, "did you lie to us all?"

The walls were closing in. Their voices blended with the crowd's cheers and the lingering echo of Christian's voice in her head. The pressure built in her chest.

She turned, pushing back through the crush of bodies, needing air before her lungs exploded. She needed to get away from the noise, the questions, the disbelief in her friends' eyes and, more than anything, she needed to get away from Christian.

She'd been used. And now she knew exactly what her Christmas wish had cost her.

CHAPTER 28

CHRISTIAN

Applause thundered in his ears, but Christian's heartbeat drowned it all out. He scanned the crowd, willing himself to smile, to look composed, like a man ready to take over a New York institution with a vision to be proud of. But his eyes flicked between faces in a growing panic.

Where was she?

He tried to speak but all he could think was that Merry wasn't anywhere to be seen. Why had his dad sprung this on him with no warning? But, as Christian looked to his dad, he knew the old man wasn't to blame. Christian should have told Merry the truth right from the very beginning. He had enjoyed being anonymous and it had cost him dearly.

There.

A flicker of movement, near the back. Shimmering dress, red hair. It was Merry, pushing through the crowd, head down, body taut like a bowstring.

No. No, no, no.

He stepped towards the edge of the platform instinctively, mic still in hand, voice faltering as he knew he couldn't run away this time.

"And of course, we couldn't have done any of this without the incredible staff." He caught himself. "Thank you. Your dedication is unmatched."

His mouth moved, but his gaze followed her, watching as she slipped out of the room without a second glance back at him. God, he'd messed this up.

He turned back to the mic, heart hammering. "Carroll's is more than a store to me, it's my family." His voice cracked, and he cleared it, forcing the rest of the sentence out. "And I'm honoured — truly honoured — to be a part of it again."

Cameras flashed and people pointed their phones at him, capturing every word he was saying. But all Christian could think was that the one person he needed to hear him most was already gone. He felt his dad's hand on the small of his back, and something inside him cracked.

He turned back to the crowd before he broke completely. He owed them too. They had been under so much pressure the last few months and he needed to tell them all it would be okay.

"I know there's been confusion around what's been going on here at Carroll's." His voice steadied, even as his heart frayed. "We've made mistakes. And I want you to hear this from me first, I'm going to fix the mess. Carroll's will be transparent from here on in."

He turned, catching his father's eye. Lewis looked as stunned as everyone else and Christian stepped off the mic and pulled him into a hug.

"I'm sorry," he said quietly into his shoulder. "For disappearing. I'll do my best for Carroll's, I promise."

Lewis squeezed his arm. "I know. I love you, son."

"I love you too, Dad." Christian nodded, then spun back to the mic. "Now, if you'll excuse me," he said, trying for levity and failing to keep the urgency from his voice, "I'm absolutely desperate for a vol-au-vent."

A chuckle rose from the crowd, but he was already off the stage, weaving through staff and well-wishers. He had something more important to chase than applause.

He burst into the hallway, scanning left and right. *Where the hell did she go?*

Then he caught sight of the elevator at the end of the corridor. The light above it pinged bright at floor ten. He took off, yanking open the stairwell door and running up to the tenth floor two steps at a time.

By the time he got there his legs were burning and his lungs were seizing painful snatches of air. He thought she'd be heading to the locker rooms to grab her bag, but he skidded out into the hallway just in time to see a door slam shut at the far end. The roof access.

Not stopping to second-guess what he was going to say when he saw her, Christian pushed through to the roof and the icy air slapped him in the face. He crossed the rooftop quickly, shoes slipping on the slick metal covers as he made for the conservatory.

She had to be in there He reached for the door just as it swung open.

"Oh!" It wasn't Merry.

Mrs Cradley stood framed in the doorway, eyes watery from the cold, braced against the snow as she rubbed her hands together briskly.

Christian froze. "Mrs Cradley."

To his utter shock, the stern-faced guardian of the employee rota smiled at him. Actually smiled.

"Well, don't just stand there gawping," she said. "Get in before your eyelashes freeze off."

He blinked. "What?"

She stepped aside, ushering him through the door. Inside, the warmth of the little glass room hit him like a memory. Two cups of hot chocolate waited on the table, clouds of whipped cream slowly melting beneath rainbow sprinkles.

Christian stared at them.

"Did you—?"

"Yes," she said, pulling a woollen hat down over her ears. "I see everything that goes on in this store. I see the duties, yes,

I see the chatter and the late arrivals, but I also see the magic. And this—" she smiled at him — "is magic."

Her eyes softened on him. "It's good to have you home, Christian."

Christian frowned. "How long have you known?"

Mrs Cradley smiled and turned to go. Then she seemed to have second thoughts.

"There's something you should know," she told him. "I saw you that day, hiding in the toys, listening to Margot and me."

Christian stiffened.

"You heard us talking," she went on. "I saw the look on your face. You thought we were scheming, didn't you? Against the store, I mean?"

Wary, he nodded once.

"We weren't." Her eyes held his. "We were talking about your father."

Christian's breath caught.

"He'd stopped listening to reason," she said simply. "Started making decisions behind closed doors. Gutting the heart of this place, piece by piece. Margot and I . . . well, we were trying to stop him before there was nothing left to save. Margot may be harsh in many ways, but she didn't want to see Carroll's sabotaged. She's given her life to this place, even if sometimes maybe it would have been better for her to have a life away from your father, if you see where I'm going?"

A gust of wind rustled her hat as she stepped fully into the doorway, silhouetted against the city skyline.

Christian stared at her, his throat tight.

"Margot . . . and Dad?" he murmured, piecing it together.

Mrs Cradley gave him a quiet, knowing smile. "As I said, Mr Carroll, I see everything. Margot loved your dad, but your dad stayed ever faithful to your mum, even when she wasn't around anymore."

Then she nodded towards the conservatory behind him. "Now, go on. It's your turn. She's in there and she's hurting. And you need to fix it."

She slipped away into the wind, leaving Christian reeling as the door clicked shut behind him with a finality that echoed in his bones.

Merry was standing by the little sofa, her back to him, shoulders shaking as she folded her dress with trembling hands. Her hair was falling from where it had been pinned up, strands tickling down her back, and she was already zipped back into her old Carroll's uniform. Reclaiming the version of herself he'd met that first day at the front door.

Her duffle bag lay open on the cushions. She lifted the dress as if it were breakable and tucked it carefully inside.

"Merry," he whispered, afraid to break the silence.

She didn't look at him. Just zipped the bag closed.

"You don't get to say my name," she said flatly, turning. Her face was blotchy, streaked with mascara, eyes blazing. "You don't get to stand there and pretend you care when all of this—" she flung a hand towards the conservatory — "was a performance."

"It wasn't. I promise, nothing about me is a performance."

"Oh, please." She bent down, grabbed the duffle bag by the handles, and threw it at him. He caught it, barely, and placed it gently on the floor.

"I don't want to be bought," she said, voice breaking. "Not with Storm dresses or goddamn whipped cream and sprinkles."

Christian's stomach dropped. "I'd never—"

"You told me you saved Devlin's life," she snapped. "I bet you were both just laughing at me behind my back. And I was an idiot to believe you. Like, what the fuck, saved Devlin's life? I blame myself for believing it."

"I actually did save his—"

"Don't," she said sharply. "Don't twist it. You embedded yourself here like some undercover billionaire, gathering information so you could take control. And I—" Her voice cracked. "I let you in. I trusted you. God, I even defended you."

"Merry, please," he said, helpless, stepping towards her.

She backed away.

"Were you even planning on leaving, or was that another ploy to get me in deeply and quickly?"

"I was leaving, I promise." Christian ran a hand through his hair. "God, this is such a mess."

"I wish you still were. I was happy before you came along. I had a simple life, a good job, friends. You've wrecked all of that. I hope you're happy with yourself."

Silence pulsed between them as Christian scrambled to find something to say that Merry would listen to. But it was too late. She was already lost to him.

"I never want to see you again," she said, with a cold finality.

CHAPTER 29

MERRY

She stormed forward, pushing open the door and blinking hard, just needing to get away before she did something more than throwing her bag at his face. Even the fact he'd caught it before it bumped his stupid, perfect nose made her blood boil.

"Were you?" His voice cut through the wind.

She stopped dead.

"What?" she asked, without turning.

"Were you actually happy?"

Now she turned, slowly, shaking her head in angry disbelief.

"Seriously?" she spat. "That's your defence? That I wasn't happy enough before you came along, so it's fine that you lied to me?"

"No." He held her gaze. "It's not fine that I lied to you. I hate that I did and I wish that I could rewind our time together and tell you who I am from the first moment we met. I can't do that. But don't lie to yourself, Merry. You say you were happy . . . but you didn't seem it."

She opened her mouth, ready to throw more words at him like sharp stabby knives in his stupid puppy-dog eyes, but none came.

"You are many thing, Merry," he went on. "Brilliant. Capable. Fierce. Hot as hell. But happy? You looked like someone who'd built a life that didn't quite fit and convinced herself to shrink into it."

Her eyes burned but she felt her shoulders slump at the weight of his words. "You don't get to say that."

"I know," he said. "Believe me, I know. The only reason I could see it in you is because I've been lying to myself too. And the only time I've ever felt real was when I was with you."

Merry blinked rapidly. Her breath caught and, for one awful second, she thought she might cry again. But she held back her tears with a deep breath and straightened her shoulders. "You should've just told me the truth."

"I know," he said again. "But I just wanted to make you happy and my fake self seemed to do that quite well. And then I was in too deep and didn't want to burst the bubble by telling the truth."

Her first instinct was pure, white-hot fury. How dare he stand there and poke holes in her reality after everything he'd done? How dare he decide that lying had been better for her? But the anger got tangled up in something else. Something that hurt more than thinking about Christian's lies.

She thought of her roommate, Clare, always leaving the groceries and the bills to her, always crying over some boy or having loud sex with another while Merry soothed and sorted and swept the pieces up behind her. She thought of the smiling, grateful shoppers who clung to her service and how she gave and gave until she had nothing left at the end of each shift. She thought of the carefully worded emails to her parents, the money transfers, the bright emojis masking exhaustion.

Was Christian right? Had she been happy or was she just really good at pretending?

Christian stepped closer, tentatively, as though he was approaching a wild cat. "You deserve better than a life you have to survive."

She stared at him, torn in two, because he had lied. But he'd also seen her in a way no one else ever had. Merry shivered as the wind curled around them, tugging at the edges of her uniform, but it was nothing compared to the storm of emotion rolling in her chest.

Christian's voice broke through it.

"When we spent time together, when you smiled at me, laughed at my jokes, I know it wasn't because of my name," he said. "Or the fact that my father owns this place. It was *me* you liked." He took a step closer. "And for the first time in my life, that mattered more than anything. I loved the fact you had no idea who I was and still wanted to spend time with me."

Merry swallowed hard.

"The date at Bryant Park," he said softly, eyes locked on hers. "That wasn't fake. Not for a second. I loved every minute of that night. The lights, the music, even the damn rain. God, Merry, I loved touching you, kissing you." Another step closer. "I still do."

Merry's heart twisted. She didn't know if she wanted to run or scream or fall into his arms. Instead, she stood perfectly still, fighting the war inside herself.

Christian shifted, rubbing his hands together, his breath misting as the cold air whirled in through the open door and the first flakes of snow started to fall beyond.

"Look, it's freezing. We don't have to stay here," he said gently. "Come with me to my hotel. It's just around the corner. We can warm up and talk properly with no interruptions."

Merry stared at him, knowing that the old her would've said no and curled up behind a wall of pride to stew. But she was so tired of pretending and of always carrying everything alone.

"No Ninja Dragon Lady?" Merry said, with a tired smile.

Christian glanced behind him at the mugs on the table that Mrs Cradley had left for them. "No Ninja Dragon Lady. She surprised me tonight, though. I don't think she's all bad."

As they made their way across the roof and back into the warmth of the tenth floor, Merry paused. Out of the corner of her eye, she thought she saw a faint glow spilling beneath the velvet curtains of the grotto.

She slowed down, frowning.

"Everything okay?" Christian asked, glancing back.

"Yeah," she muttered. "Yeah, all good."

She looked again, but the grotto was empty. It had probably just been someone locking up or a reflection from the night lighting. Still, as they walked on, she found herself glancing back one last time, wondering what she'd seen.

By the time they reached the hotel, her fingers were stinging and her cheeks felt windburned, as the snow was still falling in thick flurries. The lights from the lobby spilled a welcoming gold across the pavement, and the doorman tipped his hat as Christian led her through. Everything smelled faintly of polished wood and Christmas.

It was only when they reached the penthouse door and he pulled out the key card to usher Merry inside that she felt a jolt of realisation of what Christian really represented. The suite was vast, with floor-to-ceiling windows, a fireplace flickering gently in the corner, a towering tree in the window dressed in snowy whites and deep emeralds. The lights were low and warm.

"And now I get to see how the other half really live. Now I'm even more embarrassed about my frozen-on-the-inside windows." She let out a low whistle.

Christian laughed. "You have nothing to be embarrassed about, Merry. Some people would pay a fortune for that kind of air con. This suite is a bit much, but you looked like you needed somewhere soft to land."

God, she really did.

She followed him to a bathroom that was bigger than her whole apartment, and paused in the doorway as he lifted a glass bottle from beside the claw-footed bathtub. "Would a bubble bath help that landing?"

"Abso-freaking-lutely," she said, with no hesitation.

She knew they had important things still to talk about, but right now, Merry needed a little space to process what had happened — and for once she wasn't going to let her own stubbornness stop her from doing what she actually wanted. So, ten minutes later, she was sinking into a giant marble tub, surrounded by clouds of lavender-scented foam, her sore muscles sighing in relief. The snow-covered city glittered beyond the steamed-up windows and, in here, all was quiet and safe.

When she stepped out, wrinkled and happy and wrapped in the kind of fluffy white robe that felt like being hugged by a marshmallow, Christian was waiting for her, looking freshly out of the shower himself. His hair was damp and tousled and he was wrapped in a matching robe, tied loosely at his waist. From the delicious smells wafting around the suite, it looked like he had also been busy ordering them some room service.

"Hey, you," he said, lifting the silver lid off a tray as she padded through to the living area. "I thought you might not have eaten at the buffet, given what happened."

Merry stared wide-eyed at the tray. There were sliders, truffle fries, what looked like a tiny mac and cheese in a copper pot and a chocolate tart with a glossy top that looked indecent.

"You're incredible," she murmured, pulling on the robe and sinking into one of the sofas as Christian waited on her hand and foot. "This is incredible. Is this a normal night for you? Room service and bubble baths bigger than pools?"

He shook his head, smiling, and brought her plates of food, poured her a cup of camomile tea and, as he came to sit beside her, Merry felt like a cloud had lifted. And maybe that's why the words finally came.

"I send most of my money home," she said quietly, picking at a fry. "My sister's health isn't great and my mum is her full-time carer so she can't do paid work. Dad tries his hardest but he's spinning plates that are old and cracked and are going to smash to the floor, so I send them what I have because they don't have anyone else."

Christian didn't interrupt, though he did steal one of her truffle fries.

"I always tell myself it's fine," she went on. "That I'm lucky to finally have a job that pays okay, that I like the customers, that I'm good at it. But sometimes, when I go home at night, it's like I vanish. I eat and sleep and wake up to do it all over again. I feel like I don't really exist outside of helping other people."

He nodded slowly, eyes on hers. "You don't need to help me, Merry. We can be a team. Equals."

Her throat tightened as she looked around. "I can try to be equal to this, but you still lied to me and I need to know that I can trust you."

"I did lie." His voice was full of regret. "And I'll spend however long it takes to make that up to you and earn back your trust. But Merry . . . I meant every second we spent together. I promise you that was real, and I really don't want to lose that, especially now I'm staying in New York indefinitely. You can trust that I'm still Christian. Just a guy who loves cheesesteaks and scruffy clothes and who is learning to love Christmas again. Let me help you for a change. Give over some of that control you cling to and let me be in charge of all your worries."

"I'm not sure I can," she said quietly, fear spiralling in her chest. "I still have to send money home. My sister's care isn't cheap, and my dad . . ." She trailed off, shaking her head. "It's not like I can just stop. They need me. And what if my roommate stops paying the bills if I don't keep prompting her? We'll get chucked out, and then I—"

Christian smiled gently and put a hand on Merry's arm, stopping her from sinking further. "Merry, breathe. I know all of this is scary, but if I'm not allowed to help you now that I've outed myself as a secret billionaire, then honestly, what was the point of the whole dramatic reveal?"

Despite herself, she let out a choked laugh.

"I mean it," he said. "I'm not trying to rescue you or take over your whole life. But I am trying to stand beside you. You don't have to do it all on your own anymore, Merry. Not if you don't want to."

Her heart fluttered, traitorously hopeful at the idea she wasn't having to choose between duty and joy.

"Why me?" she asked, half-expecting the penthouse suite walls to fall down around her to reveal a hidden camera show.

Christian smiled, a slow, crooked thing that made her stomach dip.

"Well," he said, "you did headbutt me the first time you ever met me. There's a very real chance I'm still concussed."

She let out a startled laugh, and he moved closer, eyes steady on hers.

"But also because I'm falling for you, Merry Sinclair," he said quietly. "And I want you to feel like it's Christmas every day when you're with me. Good Christmas, the one you deserve."

"Does that mean you're a gift I'll get to unwrap every day too?" Merry asked, feeling a little cheeky now she was warm and fed and happy from her head to her toes.

Christian stilled. Then, slowly, he set down his whisky, eyes darkening in a way that sent a ripple through her whole body.

"I really hope so," he murmured. "But just so you know, once you unwrap me, there are no returns."

Merry laughed, but it caught in her throat as he leaned forward and slid his hand behind her neck, thumb brushing her jaw, and kissed her. He kissed her like he already knew every inch of her and couldn't wait to relearn it all, detail by delicious detail.

"You sure about this?" he asked, voice husky.

Merry nodded, tugging gently at the belt of his robe. "I know we're a few days early, but I think it's time I opened my present."

That was all the invitation he needed. He scooped her up in one swift motion and carried her towards the bedroom with a grin that melted her bones. And, as he laid her gently on the bed and leaned in again, all Merry could think was that maybe Christmas wishes really do come true.

CHAPTER 30

CHRISTIAN
CHRISTMAS EVE

Christian lingered at the foot of the giant Christmas tree for a moment longer than he should have, just watching her. Merry stood at the entrance to Carroll's in her uniform, her smile brighter than the lights on the branches behind her. She greeted every customer with a warm "Happy Christmas!" which made people beam with joy as they entered the store.

Merry by name, he thought, utterly gone for her, *and merry by nature.*

He adjusted his tie and forced himself to step away, heading up to the offices. It was his first official day at the helm of Carroll's and he wasn't too ashamed to say the nerves were real. Mrs Cradley was waiting in the corridor with her trusty clipboard tucked under her arm and a familiar air of tightly wound annoyance But she gave him a wink as he passed her and a look that said, *I may be watching you, but I'm also rooting for you.*

Christian pushed open the door to his father's office and paused on the threshold. Lewis Carroll was standing by the window, looking out over the snow-covered streets below. It was beautiful and made Fifth Avenue look like a Christmas card. It also made Christian glad of the five-minute walk across the road to work.

He stopped in his tracks at the sight. Not because of the snow, this time, but because of the sweater his dad was wearing. It was bright red, a Fair Isle pattern of reindeer and snowflakes. Lewis had worn nothing but a suit in decades.

Christian let out a surprised laugh. "Okay, who are you and what have you done with my father?"

Lewis turned with a shrug, the red sweater slightly baggy across his thin chest. "I don't know why I didn't wear this all the time," he said. "It's unbelievably comfortable." He motioned towards Christian's tie with a wry smile. "Meanwhile, you look like you can't wait to rip that off."

Christian chuckled, loosening the knot. "I'd love to, and if the big boss can wear a Christmas sweater to work, then so can I."

"I hate to break the bubble, son." Lewis nodded thoughtfully. "But you are the big boss now, and you need to keep that on. I'm just here for the free gingerbread cookie if I spend over ten dollars."

He turned and pulled out his chair from the giant desk he always sat behind. Christian smiled, expecting his dad to sit down, to start talking business. But Lewis stepped aside and gestured to the seat instead.

"I think this is yours now," he said simply.

Christian swallowed hard, a fizz of tears building in his nose.

"Dad, I . . . I don't know what to—" He shook his head. "Thank you. Really. I—"

Words failed him, so instead, he stepped forward and took the seat. Lowering himself, he felt the familiar leather, worn from years of use. Christian placed his hands on the desk, took a steadying breath and looked up at his father with a grateful smile. "I guess we should get to work."

Lewis grinned. "Lead the way, boss."

"First official decision," Christian said. "We're closing at four today. Staff deserve to get home early on Christmas Eve to be with their families."

Lewis chuckled. "I can feel the profit margins groaning already."

"Good job they're not your responsibility anymore then, isn't it?" Christian felt buoyed by the newfound friendship he was building with his father. It had been a while since they'd joked together and he vowed to do it more often.

A sharp knock sounded at the door and Lewis turned, already moving. "That's my cue. If I leave now, I think I've got time to spend ten dollars and claim my complimentary cookie."

Christian laughed. "You could just take one, you know?"

Lewis waved him off "Where's the fun in that?"

As he opened the door, Margot stood waiting on the threshold, her hair pulled into its usual no-nonsense chignon and her face looking pinched.

"Margot," Lewis said warmly, stepping aside for her. "I'll leave you in the capable hands of the man in charge."

She nodded, watching him go, then walked into the office, giving Christian a terse smile. "You wanted to see me?" she said, her words clipped.

"Sit down, Margot, please," Christian said, offering her the seat at the other side of the desk.

She perched at the very edge and sat with her hands in her lap. Christian felt a bolt of sorrow for all that she had been through.

"You've given this place everything," he said. "Even when it didn't give back."

Her face twitched, a small blossom of pink colouring her cheeks.

"I know my father wasn't always fair to you," he said, gently. "But you have worked so hard for Carroll's for as long as I can remember. We might not have some of the same views, and I will be doing what I can to make the store more ethical, but there's no doubting your heart was fully given over to Carroll's." He held out a folded envelope. Inside was a written offer of a generous retirement bonus. "You've more than earned a little sunshine."

She stared at it. "Is this your way of firing me?"

"No, Margot, it's my way of thanking you. There will always be a job here for you, if you want it. But if you're staying out of guilt or stubbornness or feelings for my father, don't. Go live your life, Margot. Go be happy."

For a moment, she said nothing. Then she sighed, softening in a way he hadn't seen before.

"I blamed you," she said, her voice thick. "For years I thought your absence broke this place, and then your dad did what he did to bring you home. I blamed you for all of it. But the truth is, it wasn't your fault. I can see why you needed to leave and your dad just lost his grip."

Christian nodded. "So did I."

Margot stood up and walked around the desk. For a moment, Christian thought she was about to hug him, but she patted his shoulder and tucked the envelope into her coat.

"If I end up on a beach with a cocktail before New Year's, I'll send you a postcard."

He smiled. "Deal."

She left, her heels clicking down the hallway like punctuation marks on the end of an era.

He had one more job to do up in the offices before he could go and join the staff on the shop floor and help with the Christmas Eve rush. They were still short of hands on deck, but Christian was hopeful that he'd be able to persuade some of the old ones back and recruit some new faces in the next few weeks. Crossing to the intercom, he flicked it on, and spoke clearly:

"Attention all staff: Carroll's will be closing at 4 p.m. today. Go home. Be with the people you love. And this year, as a special thank you, we're staying closed on Boxing Day.

This place will still be here when we all come back on the twenty-seventh."

He turned off the mic and stepped out into the corridor, feeling the buzz of happy staff around him. As he walked across the tenth floor, heading for the elevators, he caught a glimpse of Santa through the grotto doors. The old man gave Christian a knowing wink as he ho-ho-hoed at a group of excited children.

Christian grinned and shook his head, laughter bubbling up in his chest. He still had no idea how the man looked exactly the same as he had when Christian was a boy. He needed to ask him what his secret was, but he'd wait until after his queue had gone. Besides, there was something a pinch more important than Santa's skincare waiting for him on the ground floor.

On impulse, he ducked into the service closet, and there in the corner was his old janitor's trolley. He wheeled it out with a quiet laugh and rode the elevator down with it, earning a few curious glances along the way. When he stepped out on to the shop floor, the hubbub of happy shoppers wrapped around him.

Merry caught sight of him pushing the trolley and, without missing a beat, beamed and called out, "Happy Christmas, sir — and welcome to Carroll's! We hope you find exactly what you're looking for."

Christian smiled, stopping in front of her.

"I already did," he said softly.

Because the only thing more magical than Christmas at Carroll's was Merry.

EPILOGUE

CHRISTMAS EVE
ONE YEAR LATER

Merry wasn't sure what had woken her.

She lay still for a moment, listening to the hush of the early morning. Christian's arm was draped across her waist, heavy with sleep. His breathing was steady, the faintest brush of it warming her shoulder.

She sat up, yawning into the dark. It took her a moment to remember where she was — the huge bed and the Egyptian cotton sheets were still an unfamiliar luxury even after nearly a year had passed.

She'd moved in with Christian to his family home in Manhattan not long after New Year. The decision hadn't felt big at the time — one morning they were brushing their teeth side by side, and the next, she was handing back her keys and leaving behind her frozen windows and the ever-growing passive-aggressive roommate. She didn't miss that old place, but she remembered it fondly from a distance.

She leaned over and switched on the bedside lamp, blinking as the room came into focus. She had vague recollections of a loud thumping noise from outside the room. Christian rolled over and covered his head with a pillow, muttering something about waiting until morning to open her presents.

The mansion was quiet now, but a moment earlier, she could've sworn she'd heard something — like a knock or a thud from downstairs. She eased herself out of the covers, careful not to wake Christian, reached for the robe hanging from the foot of the bed, and padded out of the room.

The place was enormous — a palace, really, in the middle of New York — easily big enough for her and Christian, and Lewis, plus their family butler. Lewis was a new man, living his best life as a retiree with no responsibility except to try out all the coffee shops in Manhattan to find the best one. He was halfway through and loving it.

The mansion was big enough for her folks, too. They came to visit a lot, spending time being tourists in the city and living their happiest lives now they were free from the financial worry. Christian had flown them in from Nebraska yesterday morning, as a surprise, and Merry had screamed with joy when they'd arrived. Of all the gifts Christian had given her, the chance to spend Christmas with her family was the best of all.

Well, *almost* the best.

She cocked her head, listening for the noise that had woken her. She could hear Christian snoring gently, muttering something about mops and buckets. He'd brought back all the old Carroll's janitorial team and Merry thought he spent more time hanging out with them than he did in his office. He had a soft spot for his old colleagues. He seemed to enjoy the work, and that was something Merry loved about him. He was worth so much, she had discovered, but the money didn't change anything about the kind of man he was.

When they weren't working, they spent their time in the conservatory on the roof — which, they'd discovered, was tended lovingly by Mrs Cradley. Christian had bought her several new plants, and he and Merry delighted in watering them and pruning them together while the city busied itself below. They refrained from any extracurricular activities in there now — one almost run-in was enough. Mrs Cradley was no longer the Dragon Lady, she was just Catherine, though she still ran a tight ship and Merry still cowered a bit in her presence.

Another thumping noise echoed around the stairs, and Merry slipped down them. It wasn't quite three in the morning, and other than the occasional honking horn or siren, the city was silent. Part of her wondered if she needed to call the police, but their security system was sure to keep out intruders, wasn't it?

As quietly as she could she crept down the stairs, walking along the long, wide corridor. The noises were coming from the living room, and when she peeked around the door she couldn't quite believe what she was seeing.

There, by the Christmas tree she and Christian had chosen and decorated, stood a man, dressed all in red. Merry stared. It wasn't the real Santa, of course. It was the store Santa and, as he stood up, rubbing his back, he began to laugh.

"So, Merry," he said in his booming, friendly voice. "Do you believe in Christmas magic now?"

He adjusted his wire-rimmed spectacles and gave her the biggest, friendliest smile.

"Uh," said Merry, not quite sure what to say. She thought back to the night the previous Christmas when she'd walked into the grotto and made her wish. "I do," she said, smiling. "It came true."

"They always do," said Santa. "If you believe."

"Thank you," said Merry.

Santa smiled at her.

"I should be going," he said. "It's a busy night."

"Of course," said Merry, laughing.

She heard the creak of a stair behind her, and turned to see Lewis Carroll shuffling down them, rubbing his sleepy eyes. He seemed to have grown younger in the last couple of months, and his terrible cough had eased. She wondered if having Christian home had healed him in some way — not permanently, but maybe just enough. She looked back into the living room, but Santa was nowhere to be seen. Flecks of snow and soot drifted from the fireplace, dancing around one another.

"Can't sleep?" said Lewis as he walked up to her, smiling.

"Oh," said Merry, mystified. "I . . . I heard something. There was somebody here."

Lewis laughed.

"Dressed in red?" he asked, and Merry nodded.

"He drops by from time to time," said Lewis. "We're old friends. To be honest, he hasn't stopped by for a few years. It's nice to know he's back."

Merry opened her mouth to ask what on earth was going on, then snapped it closed again.

"Good night, Merry," Lewis said, shuffling towards the kitchen. "Or rather, good morning, in which case, Merry Christmas."

Was it magic? Or maybe just hope and love returning. But as the snow began to fall beyond the tall window, Merry smiled to herself, her heart full.

Because, whatever it was, it had made all her Christmas dreams come true.

THE END

THE CHOC LIT STORY

Established in 2009, Choc Lit is an independent, award-winning publisher dedicated to creating a delicious selection of quality women's fiction.

We have won 18 awards, including Publisher of the Year and the Romantic Novel of the Year, and have been shortlisted for countless others. In 2023, we were shortlisted for Publisher of the Year by the Romantic Novelists' Association.

All our novels are selected by genuine readers. We are proud to publish talented first-time authors, as well as established writers whose books we love introducing to a new generation of readers.

In 2023, we became a Joffe Books company. Best known for publishing a wide range of commercial fiction, Joffe Books has its roots in women's fiction. Today it is one of the largest independent publishers in the UK.

We love to hear from you, so please email us about absolutely anything bookish at choc-lit@joffebooks.com.

If you want to receive free books every Friday and hear about all our new releases, join our mailing list here: www.joffe-books.com/freebooks.